All is not as green as it seems.

Everyone seemed to be looking at something in Frankie's hand. In fact, Frankie and Sarene seemed to be at the center of the group, looking down at whatever Frankie held.

"This is no minor annoyance, Deirdre," Frankie was saying. She waved whatever she was holding in the air—it looked like a piece of notepaper. "This isn't like when Cristobal lost our luggage. This is a threat!"

George grabbed the paper from Frankie, who looked less than thrilled about giving it up. Then she ran over to Bess and me and pressed the note into my hands.

"This was taped on Frankie and Sarene's door when they went to change for dinner," George explained.

I looked down. A message was written in huge block letters.

TELL YOUR <u>NEW YORK GLOBE</u> THAT
CASA VERDE IS A SHAM. LOOK DEEPER.
AND WATCH OUT!

NANCY DREW

Available from Aladdin

CAROLYN KEENE

NANCY DREW

GIRL DETECTIVE®

GREEN-EYED MONSTER #39

**Book One in the
Eco Mystery Trilogy**

Aladdin
New York   London   Toronto   Sydney

♣ ALADDIN

An imprint of Simon & Schuster Children's Publishing Division
1230 Avenue of the Americas, New York, NY 10020
First Aladdin paperback edition December 2009
Copyright © 2009 by Simon & Schuster, Inc.
All rights reserved, including the right of reproduction in whole or
in part in any form.
NANCY DREW and colophon are registered trademarks of Simon & Schuster, Inc.
NANCY DREW: GIRL DETECTIVE is a trademark of Simon & Schuster, Inc.
ALADDIN is a trademark of Simon & Schuster, Inc., and related logo is a registered trademark of Simon & Schuster, Inc.
For information about special discounts for bulk purchases, please contact Simon & Schuster Special Sales at 1-866-506-1949 or business@simonandschuster.com.
The Simon & Schuster Speakers Bureau can bring authors to your live event. For more information or to book an event contact the Simon & Schuster Speakers Bureau at 1-866-248-3049 or visit our website at www.simonspeakers.com.
Designed by Sammy Yuen Jr.
The text of this book was set in Bembo.
Manufactured in the United States of America

10 9 8 7 6 5 4 3 2
Library of Congress Control Number 2008943894
ISBN 978-1-4169-7844-2
ISBN 978-1-4169-9828-0 (eBook)
0210 OFF

Contents

I ♥ THE EARTH

"So what exactly is a green fair?" I asked my friends Bess and George as we walked across the River Heights High School parking lot to the gymnasium entrance. "I've heard of a state fair. A science fair. Even a health fair. What's a green fair?"

Bess chuckled. "Well, it's basically like a health fair or a science fair, but with exhibits about how you can live more greenly."

George, Bess's cousin, wrinkled her nose. "Is that a word? *Greenly?*"

Bess sighed. "It is now. And you know what I mean." We reached the gymnasium doors, and Bess pulled them open and waited for us to go in. "Ecologically responsible? Environmentally friendly? However you want to say it."

Inside, I gasped at the sheer size of the fair. The entire gymnasium was filled to the brim with exhibits—from companies advertising green products, departments from the River Heights government, even kids from the local school district. Huge posters encouraged us to live green. But I could see that we were looking at only a tiny fraction of what the fair had to offer. The exhibits stretched all the way to the far end of the gymnasium, and then even farther, down the hallway.

Bess grabbed a sheet from a table to our right. "This says there are sixty more exhibitors in the cafeteria!" she cried. "Oh! And there's a cooking class for locally grown food going on right now! And you can learn how to greenify your cleaning routine! And how to convert your car to run on old cooking grease!"

George made a face. "Yeeecch."

I nodded. "That *sounds* like a good idea," I allowed, "but wouldn't you always be craving french fries?"

Bess kept reading the program. "Oh, it looks like you can only do it to a car that runs on diesel," she murmured, sounding seriously disappointed. "I guess you'll just have to stick with your hybrid, Nance."

I sighed dramatically. "Bummer."

George looked around impatiently. "Well, let's

get started," she suggested, gesturing to the first aisle. "At this rate, it will take us three hours to see everything, and I wanted to get some things done this afternoon."

Bess scoffed. "Get things done? What could be more important than saving the planet?"

George shrugged. "Cleaning up my room?" she suggested. "It's becoming a biohazard."

We paused in front of the first exhibit, where a pungent smell hit my nose.

"Ugh. What's that smell?" Bess asked quietly, suddenly looking less than enchanted by the green way of life.

"It smells like . . . garbage," complained George, placing her hand over her nose.

I shook my head. "No, it's more like . . . a farm?" I suggested, taking another sniff. I couldn't say it was pleasant, but it wasn't totally gross, either.

Suddenly the woman staffing the exhibit finished her conversation with an older couple and turned to the three of us. "Hello there," she said cheerfully. "Are you here to learn about composting in your backyard?"

Bess laughed. "Oh, *composting*!" she cried, seeming to place the smell. "We're old pros at composting, right, girls? Remember in third grade?"

Back when we were all in third grade, our teacher

had taught a section on the environment and we all learned how to compost. George laughed. "Oh, yeah. See, I've supported the environmental cause before!"

The woman, whose name tag read SANDY, smiled patiently, then opened a tall ceramic pot to show us the compost she was collecting inside. "You just save all your natural waste—vegetable peels, coffee grounds, even eggshells. Get yourself a nice composting box or pail for the winter, and let it break down naturally. Composting takes natural waste out of landfills and provides a powerful fertilizer. Do you garden?"

I nodded my head. "We do keep a small garden in the backyard."

Sandy smiled. "Great, then! Let me show you a few of the basics."

"All right, guys," George said with a sigh, glancing at her watch. "Let's keep it moving. We only have about six hundred more exhibits to check out."

"Okay, okay," I agreed, thanking the woman again and tucking the pamphlets she'd given me into my pocket. I must not have been paying much attention to where I was going, because the next thing I knew I *slammed* into a girl who was trying to get past the compost exhibit. As I began to stammer an apology, she sighed loudly.

"I'm sorry, I must not have been paying attention," I apologized.

"*Nancy?*" A familiar, not-entirely-welcome voice hit my ears, and I glanced up to see, sure enough: Deirdre.

"Deirdre," I greeted her, forcing a warm smile onto my face. "I'm surprised to see *you* here!" Deirdre Shannon has her good points, but I never would have pegged her as a girl who would care about saving the earth—especially if it meant she couldn't buy her favorite brand of mascara.

Deirdre glared at me as though I had slapped her. "I could say the same about you, Nancy."

I tried to soften my tone. "Have you been in the cafeteria yet? I hear there are tons more exhibits there."

Deirdre shook her head. "I just got here. I just had to get away from that *stanky* compost exhibit. I mean really, who wants garbage rotting in their kitchen?"

Bess, who seemed to have noticed I'd been held up, suddenly swept over. "You know, composting reduces the waste going into landfills and creates a great natural fertilizer that makes it easier for you to grow your own food," she told Deirdre. I was pretty sure she was quoting verbatim the front of one of the brochures the woman had given me, but I didn't say anything.

"Hello, Bess," Deirdre said coolly, looking about as happy to see Bess as I'd been to see Deirdre.

"Hello," George added, joining our circle. "Deirdre, I didn't know you were a budding environmentalist."

Bess giggled. "That's cute!" she said. "Get it? *Budding* environmentalist?"

George groaned, but I couldn't help but chuckle. Deirdre looked at us like we were speaking Chinese.

"Everybody who's *anybody* is embracing environmentalism these days," she told us, standing up a little straighter. "Did you know Julia Roberts built an entirely green home in Malibu, complete with solar panels on the roof and sustainable low-maintenance landscaping?"

"I did not know that," George replied simply.

"I did," Bess admitted with a little grin.

"It's all here in *Stylish Living* magazine: The Green Issue!"

George groaned.

"I have that," Bess said.

"Isn't it great?" asked Deirdre. "I mean, with so many prominent people getting involved, I figured I would be crazy not to jump on the bandwagon. Especially when you can get so many cute green products these days." She held up her bag. "Like this!"

I got a good look at Deirdre's tote bag for the first time: it was huge, made out of some kind of shiny, plasticky substance, with a fuzzy, smiling koala bear stitched onto the front. I ♥ THE EARTH! was printed across the front.

"Cute," observed Bess, glancing at the two of us with an unsure expression.

"Yeah, cute," I agreed, although something about Deirdre's budding environmentalism was rubbing me the wrong way.

George sighed. "Um, Deirdre," she began, as though she knew this was going to be a tough argument, "did you notice your bag is made out of *polyurethane*, which is not biodegradable?"

Deirdre made a face. "Polyurawhat?"

"It's also," George went on, reaching out to grab a tag from the inside of the bag and squinting at it, "made in *Bangladesh*. Do you know how far away that is, and how much fuel was probably consumed getting this bag to a store where you could buy it?"

Deirdre looked annoyed. "But *look* at it," she insisted. "It's got a koala on it. Everyone knows koalas care about the earth!"

"First of all," said George, "I don't think we can really know what koalas think. Second, I think your bag is the result of some bad designer figuring out that environmentalism is trendy and slapping a cute slogan on a *totally* ungreen product."

Deirdre pushed out her lower lip. "You're saying that my cute bag isn't green?"

George drew closer. "It's so not green, it's practically *orange,*" she replied.

Deirdre looked shocked. She shoved her *Stylish Living* back into her bag, then pulled the bag close to her, protectively stroking the fuzzy koala bear. "Your problem, George," she whispered fiercely, "is that you just don't understand the environmental *spirit.*"

With that, she turned on her heel and stalked away from us—keeping a good distance from the compost exhibit.

"Well, that was interesting," I said, pulling out my map of the fair.

"*That,*" said George, shaking her head, "is exactly what's wrong with environmentalism being trendy."

Bess sighed. "Okay, I see your point." She glanced over my shoulder. "But let's hurry! There's a lecture on the hottest organic cosmetics in fifteen minutes."

Two hours later I felt thoroughly educated on everything I could do to help save the planet—but also exhausted! We'd seen almost all of the exhibits, gotten estimates of our "carbon footprints," and taken applications for a Community Supported Agriculture (CSA) program that would supply us with fresh produce from a local farm every week during growing season.

"Ooh, look, they have honey," Bess cried happily, reading the CSA pamphlet.

"And it looks like honey is going to become harder and harder to get!" I added, thinking of an exhibit we'd just visited about the mysterious disappearance of America's honeybees. We'd reached the entrance to the gym, and I started fishing in my pocket for my car keys. "All right, kiddos," I said, "I feel green enough to head home."

"Oh, no!" Bess protested, at the same time George moaned, "Not yet!"

I turned to my friends, a puzzled look on my face. "What?"

Bess gave me a beseeching look. "We can't go yet," she coaxed. "In five minutes they're announcing the raffle winners!"

"Raffle winners?" I asked. I'd bought a couple of raffle tickets to support the high school's Environmental Club, but I really didn't care whether I won or not. I wasn't even sure what the prizes were—baskets of organic vegetables? A low-flow showerhead?

George nodded. "And I'm *dying* to win one of those laptops," she said. "You know—the Xo laptop. It's a tiny, awesome little device that was created for kids to use. It's the centerpiece of the One Laptop Per Child program—a program that aims to get every child in the world a laptop!"

Bess nodded. "That sounds pretty cool," she agreed.

"Best of all," George added, "the computers cost only a hundred ninety-nine dollars each, so people can easily sponsor a child in a developing country. But if I win the raffle . . ." She smiled. "Then I get one for the twenty dollars I spent on tickets. And the program gets a ton of money from everyone who bought raffle tickets."

"Okay," I said. "That sounds worth sticking around for."

Just then a voice came over the intercom: "Raffle winners are about to be announced. Anyone holding raffle tickets, please make your way to the auditorium!"

"That's us," said George quickly, grabbing Bess's arm and mine and herding us toward the gymnasium doors.

"We're coming, we're coming!" Bess said with an exasperated sigh. "No need to rip our arms off!"

"Sorry," George said, biting her lip. "But—um—could you move a little faster?"

With George prodding us the whole way, we made our way into the crowd heading for the auditorium. There we took a seat in the third row, "nice and close to the stage for when I win my laptop," George explained.

Looking around at all the filled seats, I was impressed. It looked like the town of River Heights really had come out en masse to the fair today. Hundreds of people fished out their raffle tickets, eagerly looking up at the stage.

After a few minutes, a blond, middle-aged woman who introduced herself as Julie, the owner of River Heights's organic food co-op, stepped up to begin announcing the prize winners and the prizes—everything from organic cosmetics to bamboo sheets to dinner for two at a local vegan restaurant. But as the announcements wore on, the prizes seemed to get bigger. And George, sitting next to me, began to positively bounce with excitement.

"Ooh, Nance, I haven't won anything yet!" she cried excitedly. "You know what that means! It means my name is still in there!"

Just then the woman at the podium called out, "And now, the winner of the Xo laptop, from the One Laptop Per Child program . . ."

George squeezed my hand and Bess's at the same time.

Bess shot her a stunned look. "George," she observed, "I've never seen you like this! You're acting like *me*."

"I know," George whispered, unable to take her eyes off the stage, "and believe me, I'm just as worried about it as you are."

"Kendra Jung!" the woman announced, and polite applause filled the auditorium as a young girl moved forward to accept her prize.

Immediately George's hands went slack, and she leaned back in the chair, looking exhausted. "Ugh," she muttered.

"Sorry, George," Bess said encouragingly, squeezing her cousin's shoulder. "You'll get one some other way."

I nodded, patting George's other shoulder. "And just think—your twenty dollars will go to help save the planet."

George closed her eyes and sat up, rubbing her temples. "I know," she admitted. "I know, I know. It's all good."

"And now!" the announcer continued, pulling my attention back to the stage. "The winners of our two *grand prize* packages!"

"What's the grand prize?" I whispered to George.

She shrugged. "I dunno. A trip to some spa or something? I was only interested in the laptop."

The announcer went on, "An all-expenses-paid eco-tour of Costa Rica!"

"Oh, wow!" Bess whispered, poking her cousin's arm. "That would be amazing, wouldn't it? Costa Rica is supposed to be so beautiful. I think Charlize Theron went there last year!"

George shrugged. "Well, Charlize would know," she deadpanned. "I'm sure it would be beautiful, if I were having any luck today."

The announcer plucked a raffle ticket out of the huge basket she'd been using and announced cheerfully, "GEORGE FAYNE!"

Bess's mouth dropped open. We both turned to George, who was frozen, her head still in her hands.

"Did she just say . . . me?" she asked.

I nodded. "George, get up there! You just won a trip to Costa Rica!"

George shook her head as if to clear it, and a slow smile appeared across her face. "I just won a trip to Costa Rica!" she gasped.

"That's right!" cried Bess, trying to prod her out of her seat. "And when you're deciding who to bring, just remember who made you come to this green fair in the first place!"

Bess and I both chuckled as George made her shell-shocked way up onto the stage. The announcer reached into the basket again and plucked out another ticket, then moved toward the microphone to announce, "And the other winner is . . . Deirdre Shannon!"

"AAHHHHHHHHH!" A sharp-pitched scream rose from the back of the auditorium, and I could see Deirdre leaping out of her seat and trampling over the people in her row to get to the aisle, which she promptly ran down. "Oh my gosh! AAAAH! I WON!"

George, who had just taken a folder from the announcer that contained all her trip details, looked back at us with an *uh-oh* expression. A vacation to Costa Rica with Deirdre? Probably not what she had in mind.

"Oh, no," breathed Bess, clearly thinking the same thing.

I couldn't help but laugh. "Just think, Bess," I said encouragingly. "Vacationing with Deirdre will make the trip seem even longer!"

CASA VERDE

As it turned out, I was going to be able to see up close and personal just how Deirdre reacted to Costa Rican wildlife. Bess and George insisted that I come with them. "We're the three musketeers!" Bess had cried, and George had agreed, "It's true, Nance—it won't be the same without you." So three weeks later I found myself in seat 16B on Flight 171 to San José, trying to keep George's sleeping head from falling into my lap and listening to Bess squeal about the items available in the *SkyMall* catalog.

"Oh my gosh, did you *see* this, Nance?" she asked, shoving the worn catalog under my nose. "You can grow an entire vegetable garden in your kitchen! With no soil!"

"You know, Bess, you can grow an entire vegetable garden in your *backyard*," I pointed out. "And that doesn't require a two-hundred-dollar piece of techno-junk."

Bess yanked her catalog back. "You sound like *George*," she accused. "Why don't you wake her up, by the way? We're going to land in about half an hour."

"Why don't *you* wake her up?" I volleyed back. We both knew that George was not exactly Mary Sunshine when she first got up.

Bess glanced up from the catalog, then quickly away. "Well, never mind," she muttered, energetically flipping a few pages. "She'll wake up when we land, anyway."

Just then the pilot made the announcement that we would be starting our descent into the San José area, and everyone should make their way back to their seats. Behind us, Deirdre had been chatting with her cousin, Kat, whom she'd brought along as her guest, but after the announcement, Kat squealed, "Ooh—I think I'd better make my way back to first class." As we'd learned before the plane boarded, Kat had paid to upgrade herself to a first-class seat.

Now she shimmied by us in the aisle, pausing when she met my eye. "Oh, look at you three!" she cried in a delighted voice. "Aren't you *cozy*."

Pushing George's head back up to my shoulder from my chest, I forced a smile. "Well, it's no first class," I admitted.

Kat chuckled. "Right. You know, personally, I don't mind flying coach, but my dog, you know, Pretty Boy? He gets claustrophobic."

I nodded, not sure what to say to that. At the airport we'd learned that Kat was from Los Angeles and made a nice salary working as an extra in movies and TV shows. She claimed to know hundreds of celebrities, though the best story she'd shared with us so far was about standing behind Howie Mandel in the line at Starbucks. And she'd completed "a ton" of paperwork and gone through lots of effort to bring her toy Chihuahua, Pretty Boy, to Costa Rica with her. "We're totally codependent," she'd explained to us as Pretty Boy, wearing a light blue sequined tuxedo, gnawed on her hair. "Without me around, he just spins in circles and cries all day. He doesn't even get dressed."

"Oh, well." Kat shrugged now, adjusting her T-shirt. "I'd better get back to him. I left him with a stewardess, but he was acting a little grumpy, so . . ."

I thought I heard a growl from the front of the plane, and Kat took off.

Bess, who'd kept her focus on her catalog that

whole time, put it down and watched Kat slip through the curtain to first class. "That dog bit me twice just walking down the jetway to board the plane," she recalled.

I nodded. "Kat says his doggie therapist has been working on his aggression issues."

Bess pursed her lips. "I am not dogsitting that dog," she said, slipping her catalog into the pocket on the seat in front of her. "That's all I'm saying."

Forty minutes later Bess, a very grumpy George, Deirdre, Kat, and I stumbled out of the secure part of the San José airport.

"Do we have any idea what this guy looks like?" George asked, rubbing her eyes.

"They told me he'd have a sign," Deirdre replied, and we all craned our necks, searching the crowd.

"Oh! There he is," squealed Kat, running over to a tall, dark-haired man who stood over by the currency exchange stall. He was holding a sign that said GEORGE FAYNE, DEIRDRE SHANNON, and he seemed to be searching for us just as energetically as we were searching for him.

We all followed Kat over to the man. "Are you . . . Christopher?" she was asking. "No, wait, that's not right. Christmas? Chris—"

"Cristobal?" said the man smoothly. "Yes, that's

me! And I take it you are the lovely ladies I will be hosting at Casa Verde this week?"

"We are," said George sleepily, looking surprised. "Are you Cristobal *Arrojo?* Owner of Casa Verde?"

Cristobal nodded proudly. "Co-owner, with my brother," he explained. "Perhaps you are surprised that I'm here, at the airport, but it's very important to Enrique and me that Casa Verde maintain that personal touch." As he spoke, he led us over to the baggage claim area, where suitcases were already whirring by on a conveyor belt. "When you stay with us," he added, sweeping past Kat to grab a pink suitcase that she'd been reaching for, "you are like family, *sí?* Here you are, *bonita.*"

He handed Kat her suitcase, and she practically swooned.

"Oh!" Cristobal cried, moving closer to the blue satin carrier that held a super-cranky Pretty Boy. "And who is this, may I ask?"

"That's my dog, Pretty Boy," Kat explained with a smile. "He travels with me everywhere." As she spoke, Pretty Boy let out a deep growl that seemed far too loud to be coming from such a tiny animal.

"Ah, yes," Cristobal replied, looking a little surprised. "I guess—I guess we can accept pets this one time."

Kat tossed her long, platinum blond hair. "He's

really not so much a *pet* as a *companion*."

"Of course," agreed Cristobal, turning to retrieve another suitcase, which belonged to Bess. "Well, let me tell you a little bit about Casa Verde, where you'll be staying, okay?"

"Great!" Bess cried, clearly excited. Over the last couple of weeks, we'd pored over the brochures and websites for the new family-style green resort, eager to see what it looked like in person. Even George had been impressed by Casa Verde's green credentials—they really were a state-of-the-art eco-resort.

"Casa Verde," Cristobal explained, "was once, and is once again, a working coffee plantation. For decades plantation workers harvested coffee beans there, selling them to roasters and distributors all around the world."

Deirdre nodded. "I love Costa Rican coffee," she broke in. "It's one of your largest exports, right?"

"Right." Cristobal reached to grab George's suitcase. "The rain forest climate is excellent for growing coffee. But years ago the Via Verde coffee plantation fell on hard times and closed its doors. And just last July, my brother Enrique and I stumbled on the site."

He turned to us and smiled. "Wait till you see it. Up on a hillside, with beautiful views of the surrounding hills and rain forest. It is a little piece of heaven, right here on earth."

I glanced at Bess and grinned, even more eager to see the resort.

"Enrique and I purchased the land and renovated the old plantation house into a comfortable, luxurious, and completely ecologically friendly guest house with ten rooms," he went on. "We then consulted with some environmental scientists and veterinarians to create beautiful gardens and a nature preserve right on our land. We take in wild animals in need of a new home and give them an ideal environment to thrive in. We have a full-time veterinary staff of two. You can all explore the preserve when we get back—there are three hiking trails that take you on nice tours of the land."

"Wow," murmured Kat. I noticed that she'd removed Pretty Boy from his carrier and was now nestling him in the crook of her arm. "I can't wait to see it!"

Cristobal smiled, grabbing our last suitcase. "I can't wait for you to see it," he replied. "You girls must know, we are just opening this weekend, and you will be our first guests."

George nodded. "We're honored," she told the resort owner, seeming to shake off the last vestiges of sleepiness.

"But first," Cristobal announced, checking his watch, "we must wait for a few more guests."

Kat scrunched up her eyebrows. "A few more guests?" she asked, clearly disappointed. "How many? And how long do we have to wait?"

Cristobal looked apologetic. "As I said, we are just opening this weekend," he went on. "And along with donating your vacations to help environmental causes, we invited just a few journalists to experience our resort."

"A press tour?" Bess asked. "You mean we're part of a press tour?"

"What's that?" Deirdre asked Bess, looking nonplussed.

Bess shrugged lightly. "It's when a local resort or tour company or whatever gives free vacations to a bunch of journalists," she replied. "In return, those journalists will write about the resort for their newspaper or magazine, and hopefully drive some tourists to check it out themselves."

Cristobal nodded. "Right," he agreed. "We build— how do you say it—buss?"

Bess chuckled. "*Buzz,* I think," she corrected.

"What time are the journalists arriving?" George asked.

Cristobal smiled. "There is a flight from New York arriving right now," he replied. "All our writers are on that. They should come down any minute."

Five minutes later the first journalist arrived. A tall, slim, angular woman of about twenty-five stepped off the escalator and, after looking around for a few seconds, made a beeline to Cristobal and his sign. She had short, light red hair tied back in a green and white scarf, and she wore a neat green sweater with pressed white pants. She was trailed by an equally tall, but slightly curvier woman about the same age, with long, wavy dark hair, wearing a long navy sundress.

"I'm Frankie Gundersen," the first woman said coolly to Cristobal. "From the *New York Globe*? And this is my guest, Sarene Neuman."

Sarene flashed a brief smile and shook Cristobal's hand. "Charmed," she said shortly.

"You work for the *New York Globe*?" Bess asked Frankie, smiling warmly. "That must be so exciting."

"It is," Frankie said curtly, looking Bess up and down. "You are?"

Bess held out her hand. "Oh, I'm Bess Marvin. My cousin George Fayne won this free eco-tour at a green fair at our hometown high school." She gestured at Deirdre. "Deirdre won one too, and she brought along her cousin Kat. George and I brought along our best friend, Nancy Drew."

Frankie followed Bess's introductions, taking in George, Deirdre, Kat, and finally me. She didn't look terribly impressed by any of us. "Well," she said with a little sigh, as though Bess's introduction had tired her out. "What are you, around thirteen?"

Bess frowned, and I could tell she was about to correct Frankie, but suddenly George seemed to wake up and turned to Frankie's friend with a curious expression.

"Sarene Neuman," she said, looking thoughtful. "Why do I know that name? Do you write for the *Globe* too?"

"Oh, no," Sarene replied with a little chuckle. "I don't know how Frankie does it. I write books, actually."

"Do you?" asked Deirdre, moving closer. "What kind of thing do you write? Romance? Mystery?"

Sarene shook her head distastefully. "Nonfiction," she said simply.

"*That's* it!" cried George, grinning. "You wrote *Up the River and Down*, right? The book about the life cycle of salmon that won that big award? I read that!"

Sarene's gaze flickered back to George, surprise coloring her pretty features. "*You* read my book?"

George nodded. "I think it's really interesting," she replied, "how you talked about how global warming is really impacting the salmon industry. I never thought about it that way."

Sarene still looked mystified. "Did you have to read it for school or something?"

George shook her head, looking a little annoyed. "I just borrowed it from the library and read it," she replied. "I like biology and environmental science."

Sarene still looked a little surprised, but she just sniffed and fished out a PDA from her pocket, turning it on. "If you liked it so much, you should buy a copy," she advised, then held the phone to her ear. "Oh, I have three voice mails!" She walked away.

George turned slowly back to Bess and me. I could tell from her expression that she was rethinking her Sarene Neuman fandom. "Did you see that?" she hissed.

I nodded. "Maybe she's just really jet-lagged?"

Bess snickered. "Maybe she's just really *mean*," she whispered.

I sighed. "I hope not," I said, "because like it or not, we're stuck on a tour with these people for another seven days."

George shrugged. "Maybe they'll warm up."

Just then a middle-aged woman ran over to Cristobal, pulling a sweet-faced, pigtail-wearing girl of about eight years old behind her. "Are you Cristobal?" she asked. "Have I found you?"

"Indeed you have," Cristobal said with a warm smile. "You are?"

"Hildy Kent," the woman replied, noticing the rest of us behind Cristobal and flashing us all a smile. "Freelance travel writer. And this is my daughter, Robin."

Robin was apparently a little shy, because her mom's introduction led her to try to hide behind Hildy's huge purse. Still, she flashed a mischievous smile at me when I caught her eye. At least she was nicer than Frankie or Sarene!

"Qué bonita!" Cristobal enthused, winking at the little girl. "This is your daughter? I thought perhaps you were sisters."

Robin let out a high-pitched giggle, as a tall, slim, dark-haired woman approached with a well-toned guy wearing a crew cut.

"You're Cristobal?" she asked, sliding a pair of huge sunglasses back on her head and smiling nervously.

"I am," he replied, glancing down at his list. "And are you . . . Poppy LeVeau, from *Stylish Living* magazine?"

Ouch. I frowned at Bess, who'd just elbowed me in the side, really hard. "Did you hear that?" she whispered.

I nodded. "Yeah, your favorite magazine."

Bess grinned dreamily. "I wonder if she's ever met Angelina Jolie."

Next to us, George sighed. "This is going to be a long trip."

Three hours later the eleven of us guests and all our luggage (all twenty-three pieces!) pulled into the driveway to Casa Verde, which was located outside the city in the town of San Isidro. We were traveling in a small, comfortable bus that Cristobal explained ran on electric power. I was sitting in my own seat, with Bess and George behind me, and I had opened my window to let in the balmy tropical breeze. Already I was warming up to Costa Rica. Even the air smelled amazing—a fragrant blend of tropical flowers, fruits, and earth.

The driveway snaked up a hill through a lush, deep green tropical forest.

"Nancy! Look!" George cried, poking me, but by the time I'd looked where her finger had been pointing, nothing was there.

"It was a monkey," George explained in an amazed voice. "I saw a monkey. Just hanging around in the trees by our hotel."

I grinned. "Welcome to Costa Rica," I said.

She laughed, looking really excited. "I guess so."

After a few minutes, the rain forest parted and we could see a large, low, whitewashed mansion trimmed with dark wood. Bright yellow canopies shaded a small set of steps that led to an open-air lobby. Inside, I spotted a dark wood reception desk and a small sitting area with comfy-looking chairs.

"This is it, ladies . . . and gentleman!" Cristobal laughed, glancing back at Poppy's beau, who we'd learned was named Adam. "Welcome to Casa Verde!"

We all roused ourselves out of the bus and stumbled into the lobby as though we were entering a dream. I could see that the windows on the opposite side of the house had a truly amazing view: Deep blue sky gave way to cool, cloud-topped violet hills, which gradually led down to a huge, overflowing tropical garden. I could see hiking trails leading far into the garden, and probably to the nature preserve beyond.

George stepped next to me, then reached out, took my lower jaw, and closed my mouth. I realized that I'd just been standing there staring with my mouth wide open. "It's pretty amazing, isn't it?" she asked.

I shook my head, unable to put what I was seeing into words. "It's like . . . *planet Earth* is welcoming us," I murmured, unable to tear my eyes off the window. "I don't know whether I've ever seen a place so beautiful."

Cristobal entered the lobby, holding out his arms. "Welcome, welcome, everybody!" he said again. "In about an hour, we will meet through that doorway, in the dining room, for a fresh, organic, locally grown

dinner made by my amazing chef of a brother, Enrique."
He smiled. "For now, everyone, please, explore the
grounds a bit and try to rest from your long journeys.
At the desk I have the list of room assignments, and I'll
be happy to tell you each where you'll be staying."

Bess walked up to George and me, gawking at the
view from the window. "Wow," she breathed. "Guys,
this is amazing. I don't think I could relax in the room
right now. I'm too excited!"

"Me too," I agreed. "Want to go for a walk?"

Quickly George got our room assignment and
keys from Cristobal, and we shoved them in our
pockets and headed out the back door to the gardens.
There we were even further amazed by the beauty of
the resort.

"It's like a dream garden," Bess observed, leaning
close to a trumpet-shaped white flower and taking a
whiff. "I can hardly believe it's real!"

The three of us strolled along what a sign indicated
was the shortest hiking path, at 2.3 kilometers. Slowly
we left the cultivated garden and entered a more
wild-looking area of rain forest.

"We must be getting to the preserve," said George.

Just then there was a rustling in the trees above,
and Bess gasped and pointed. "Did you see that?"

"A monkey!" I cried happily, amazed to be in the
company of such exotic wildlife.

"A *squirrel* monkey," a high, accented voice piped up behind us, and we all jumped a little at the intrusion.

I turned to face a young, friendly-looking woman in a blue polo shirt and pressed khakis. She was smiling and holding a bucket of water, clearly on her way somewhere. "Are you the new guests?" she asked.

"We are," said Bess cheerfully. "Do you work at the resort?"

The woman nodded, her ponytail bobbing behind her. "My name is Sara," she greeted us. "I'm the veterinary assistant here—I work with Alicia, the veterinarian." She looked at us a little closer. "Are you writers? This is a press tour, no?"

"No," replied George. "I mean, yes, it is a press tour, but we're not reporters. I actually won this vacation at an environmental fair in my town."

"Oh," Sara said, looking a little disappointed. "I had hoped that the American journalists would write about our resort for their newspapers."

"Oh, they will," I assured her, thinking that Sara must be concerned about her new employer's future. "There are lots of writers on the trip. We just don't happen to be part of them."

Sara nodded, looking happier. "Good." She looked down at the bucket she was carrying. "Well, I have to get this medicine down to the veterinary office. If you have any questions about the animals you see, please let me know."

We thanked Sara and moved aside to let her pass us. After another half hour or so, we had walked the entire hiking path and seen lizards, frogs, and colorful birds, in addition to a few more monkeys. We walked back up the hill toward the resort, suddenly feeling tired.

"I think it just hit me," Bess murmured. "Getting up early for the flight, plus jet lag."

"I'm ready for dinner, for sure," I agreed. "And this might be an early night for me, too."

George smirked. "You mean we can't party all night with the monkeys?" she asked. "What kind of fun are you guys?"

Inside, most of our tour had already gathered in the dining room. They stood around in groups, chatting. A pretty teenage girl came out of the kitchen and approached one group of guests.

"Oh, look." Deirdre smirked as we walked into the room. "The little wanderers have returned!"

I smiled. "Have you guys explored the grounds at all?" I asked, looking from Deirdre to Kat, who still had Pretty Boy cradled in her arms.

"We explored the pool," Kat replied enthusiastically. "Have you seen it? It's on the way to the coffee plants, and totally amazing! Fresh water, with a little waterfall . . ."

"And *totally* environmentally friendly," Deirdre added, as if suddenly remembering the resort's focus.

"That's great," Bess said. "How do you get there?"

Kat gestured off to the side of the inn. "When you go out the front door, follow the path to your left."

The pretty teenager had been going from group to group, scribbling something down on a pad of paper, and now she left Poppy and Adam to come over to the five of us. "Good evening!" she said, a warm smile on her face.

"Boo-ay-nas tar-days," Kat replied, overenunciating each syllable.

The girl nodded. "I'm Juliana," she introduced herself. "I am the daughter of Enrique, the chef."

"Oh, right," George replied, smiling at the girl. "So you're Cristobal's niece?"

"Yes," Juliana said cheerfully. "After school, I help out my father in the kitchen, and I'll be serving you tonight. Welcome to Casa Verde!"

"Oh, thank you," said Bess.

"Are you journalists?" Juliana asked us eagerly, looking at each of us in turn. "You all look so young!"

"Oh, no, we're not writers." I chuckled. "We snuck onto the press tour by winning these vacations. We're probably closer to your age."

Juliana nodded. "Well, welcome!" she repeated. "I am so excited for the opening of Casa Verde. My father and Uncle Cristobal have worked so hard. And I think the resort is beautiful."

Bess grinned. "Well, I think we all *totally* agree."

Juliana took our drink orders, and a few minutes later all eleven of us sat down at a big table for dinner. Then a short, portly gentleman with a small mustache came out of the kitchen with a big plate of roasted chicken and a smaller bowl of black beans. He looked around our table nervously, as though uncomfortable being the center of so much attention.

"Welcome to Casa Verde!" he said a little awkwardly, looking down at the food he'd prepared. "I am Enrique Arrojo, Cristobal's brother. I hope . . . ah . . . I hope . . ."

Juliana took the bowl of beans from her father and smoothly placed it on the table, smiling. "We hope you're as excited by this meal as we were to prepare it for you," she finished.

Enrique smiled at her. "*Sí,*" he agreed, then glanced at all of us. "We are very happy to have our first guests. Please, enjoy." With that, he went back into the kitchen.

Dinner was delicious, and it was a lot of fun to talk casually with our fellow travelers, the journalists and their guests. Sarene and Frankie still seemed a little standoffish, but even they had to smile at some of young Robin's observations, or Poppy's amazing stories about interviewing celebrities and attending Hollywood parties.

"Maybe we know some of the same people," Kat suggested, leaning over the table toward Poppy and squishing Pretty Boy, who was still in her lap, in the process. He squealed, and she leaped back. "Oh, baby!" she cooed, stroking his back. "Anyway—*I* know a few celebrities myself. I make my living as an extra."

"Oh," Poppy replied, looking mildly interested. "So you're an aspiring actress? Do you have your SAG card?"

"No," Kat sniffed, as though this were a sore point for her. "I'm not part of the Screen Actors Guild because I've never had my own lines. But I've worked with lots of amazing people."

Poppy nodded encouragingly. "Like?"

Kat grinned. "I was just on this horror movie— *Attack of the Moldy Jell-O?*" She paused to wait for recognition, but nobody spoke up. "Anyway, remember that guy Juan, the one who was the runner-up on *America's Next Top Celebrity Assistant?* He was the one who brought a two-percent latte instead of skim?"

Poppy looked lost. "Well, I didn't really watch that show."

Kat nodded. "Well, he's in it. He's *huge* right now. And we, like, got into this whole conversation by craft services about how hot it was."

Poppy nodded, smiling a friendly smile. "Well, we did a feature on the new *Real Life* house."

That sparked a long discussion of that show: how long people had watched it, whether anybody watched it anymore, and what people thought of the most recent cast. By the time Enrique brought out a tray of flan, I felt like I was sitting at a table with my closest friends—aside from Frankie and Sarene, maybe.

Just after we'd dug into the flan, I spotted Cristobal dashing through the dining room and into the kitchen. I could vaguely hear upset voices back there, but it was hard to hear over the ongoing chatter at the table. I caught George's eye, and she glanced back at the kitchen and shrugged. I shrugged back. *Important brother business?* I mouthed to her.

After a few minutes, Cristobal emerged from the kitchen. He turned immediately to all of us at the table, and I could tell from his expression that something was wrong. He looked angry, a little uncomfortable, and more than anything, frustrated—that kind of frustrated expression you get when you really don't understand something that just happened.

"Um, ladies," he called, then sheepishly glanced at

Adam, "and gentleman! I'm afraid I have some bad news."

We all glanced at one another, no doubt wondering what could go wrong in this little piece of heaven. "What is it?" asked Hildy. "You can tell us. We're tougher than we look."

Cristobal sighed. "Of this, I am sure. But the problem is . . . your luggage."

Frankie suddenly piped up, looking worried, "What about our luggage?"

Cristobal glanced back at the kitchen again, and then to the lobby. "It seems to be . . ." He paused, and we looked expectantly at him. What could possibly have happened?

"Missing."

LOOK DEEPER

The next morning Bess and George and I changed out of the oversize T-shirts we'd been given to sleep in (Cristobal hadn't specified, but from the sizes and degree of wear, we were pretty sure they belonged to him or Enrique) and back into the clothes we'd worn on the plane.

"Ugh," Bess complained. "I can't wait until they find our luggage! It feels so yucky to be stuck in these same clothes."

I nodded, "brushing" my teeth with my finger in the bathroom. "Well, Cristobal said that if they don't find it by this afternoon, Casa Verde will give us each a one-hundred-dollar budget to buy some new clothes and toiletries."

George sighed, reaching around me to grab the hairbrush Poppy had loaned us from her purse. "I'd feel terrible taking money out of their pockets," she said, "but I can't imagine what happened to our suitcases! Cristobal said they were all loaded into the lobby, and then they just—disappeared."

"I know," Bess said with a nod, looking concerned. "It's pretty weird."

I shrugged. "Maybe it was just a misunderstanding, or someone's idea of a prank," I suggested.

"Who would be playing a prank on the resort's first guests?" asked George, looking skeptical.

I sighed. "Do you have any other theories?"

George frowned and shook her head. "Bess is right," she said. "This is *very* weird."

I took the hairbrush from her, pulled it quickly through my own hair, and then pulled my hair back into a ponytail with a holder I'd had in my pocket the day before. "Let's just try to forget about it and have fun," I told the other two. "I can't wait to check out InBioParque today!"

We'd been asked to meet back in the lobby at nine A.M. so we could all have a light breakfast, then get back into the bus so Cristobal could bring us to a popular local attraction. InBioParque was an amusement park that promised to bring its visitors up close and personal with nature. I was eager to check it out with the group—and to learn more about the local flora and fauna.

"Buenos dias, señoritas!" Cristobal greeted us with a big smile as we strolled into the dining room. "Please, have some fruit and fresh-baked pastries, courtesy of Enrique. There is also fresh coffee, grown right here at Casa Verde!"

"Wow," I replied, looking over at the very popular coffee station. "I don't usually drink coffee, but I might have to make an exception for that."

Cristobal beamed. "Please, enjoy," he said coaxingly. "I am so sorry about your luggage. The least we can do is provide you with a delicious breakfast."

And delicious it was. The coffee was amazingly smooth and rich, and the pastries, filled with mild cheese and a fruity paste that Cristobal told us was guava, were amazing. After we finished, we all climbed back onto the bus, where Cristobal introduced us to a young guy named Pedro, Casa Verde's driver.

"Pedro will be safely transporting us all over Costa Rica," Cristobal explained to us, "leaving me free to answer questions and talk about the sights."

A couple hours of driving later—and driving seemed like a challenge in Costa Rica, with lots of narrow country roads—we arrived at InBioParque.

"Here you will be able to see much of Costa

Rica's amazing biodiversity," Cristobal explained as we entered the park. "With our unique climate and topography, Costa Rica has always been blessed with a rich array of plants and animals. But in 1948, after our most recent civil war, President José Figueres Ferrer decided to make us the first nation to abolish our military. The military budget was then invested in security, culture, and education. As a nation, we also made natural conservation a top priority." He paused. "Today, twenty-seven percent of our country is protected land. As a result, we have protected countless species and encouraged an unparalleled level of biodiversity. And we have also expanded our tourism industry, pioneering the concept of ecotourism."

Kat giggled. "Well, we know that, silly," she told Cristobal, stroking Pretty Boy, who rested in the crook of her arm. "After all, we're your first ecotourists!"

Cristobal smiled. He then took us to the Butterfly Garden, where we gawked at the beauty of fifteen different species of butterflies. Bright orange, black, blue, and red wings fluttered all over the area, getting nearly close enough for us to touch.

"Oh, my goodness," said Deirdre. "They're so gorgeous, I want to take them home with me!"

Cristobal shook his head. "That would be a very bad idea," he replied. "Even touching these delicate creatures' wings can cause them to wither and die. It's best to admire them from a distance."

When we were finished at the Butterfly Garden, Cristobal announced that he was leading us on a hike through the park's trails. "Keep your eyes open," he advised us. "We'll likely be joined by lots of animal companions. We might see sloths, turtles, white-tailed deer, iguanas, or caimans. And that's not to mention the five hundred eighty-three species of plants!"

Bess, George, and I followed along eagerly, everyone in our group excitedly pointing out different birds and animals they spotted along the way.

"This is incredible," George breathed as we watched a white-tailed deer take a long drink from a tiny stream. "I mean, I know I was skeptical about the whole ecotourism thing, but this is a once-in-a-lifetime experience."

Bess smirked. "Well, you know I'm not the type to say, 'I told you so.'"

"You're not?" I asked, laughing.

Bess giggled. "Oh, okay," she replied, turning to face George. "I told you so."

But George looked too happy to be even a little bothered by this. "I know," she said simply. "And I'm glad you were right. This is going to be an amazing trip."

In addition to the trails and Butterfly Garden,

InBioParque also had a working farm and a lagoon with an underground aquarium that allowed us to see the creatures that lived in the lagoon up close. When lunchtime rolled around, Cristobal treated us to a quick snack at the park's café. Then he looked at his watch and frowned.

"Oh, my guests," he said with a sigh, "I know we are having fun here. But while you were eating, I called Enrique to check up on your luggage."

We all pricked up our ears, eager to hear whether we'd have clean clothes to change into when we got back to the resort. But Cristobal didn't look happy.

"It is still missing," he went on. "And I simply cannot let you go on feeling uncomfortable in our care. I think I must give you each one hundred dollars to spend on new clothes, and we must take the rest of the afternoon to go shopping."

I knew Bess was a champion shopper, but even she looked concerned about this. "But I don't understand," she spoke up. "What could have happened to all our luggage?"

"Yeah," Frankie piped up, looking terribly annoyed. "Twenty-three suitcases don't just get up and walk away."

Cristobal looked uneasy. "It is odd, I know," he replied, looking down at his hands. "But all I can say is that I hope to make this right. We take full responsibility. And we will help you get some new belongings to replace the old."

Hildy smiled and reached out to pat Cristobal's hand. "After what you've shown us today," she told him, "you've made it very hard to be upset with you. Robin and I trust you, Cristobal."

Cristobal looked grateful. "Thank you," he replied. "I appreciate that."

Robin suddenly spoke up, her high-pitched voice immediately lightening the mood. "I saw a turtle," she announced proudly, referring to a beautiful green sea turtle we'd seen in the lagoon.

Hildy chuckled. "Yes, you did," she said, patting her daughter on the head. "And once we get some new clothes to change into, Cristobal is going to show us much more."

Later that evening, Bess and I unpacked our new jeans and T-shirts and then slipped out to explore the grounds some more while George took, as she called it, "a quick siesta." The air was warm and balmy, with a comfortable breeze blowing through the trees. We checked out the freshwater pool Kat had mentioned—which was just as gorgeous as she'd told us, and crowded with Kat, Deirdre, Frankie, and Sarene—and then looped around back to the trails we'd started to explore the day before.

"Let's choose another one," Bess suggested, looking down at the map that was posted at the head of the trails. "We have ninety minutes before dinner. I bet we could make the loop around on the Coco Trail, here." She pointed.

I shrugged. "Sure, let's give it a try." I figured that as long as we kept our eyes on our watches and started to head back when it was getting late, we'd be fine.

As we walked farther down the trail, the lush gardens gave way to more wild-looking forest. We spotted another squirrel monkey and were able to identify some of the birds and lizards we saw, using the names we'd learned at the park earlier.

After a few minutes, Bess suddenly paused on a small bridge and stared down the stream.

"Bess," I prodded, nudging her. "Are you zoning out on me?"

She shook her head, turning to me briefly, and then pointed where she'd been staring. "Do you see that?" she asked.

I followed her gaze. The sun was just beginning to dip below the horizon, so it was hard to make out the object of interest in the pale blue light. But as soon as I saw it, I gasped.

"You see it?" Bess asked, alarm in her voice. "It's weird, right?"

The sign where the trail maps were posted in the garden had clearly stated PLEASE STAY ON THE TRAIL. And we'd learned earlier today about the importance of "not interfering with nature," as Cristobal put it. It was fine to enjoy the beautiful plants and exotic animals from a distance. But get too close, and you might be putting them in danger and not even know it.

Still, now, what I was seeing was important enough for me to back off the bridge and step off the trail. I walked a few yards in the spongy, leaf-covered earth, over to a large stone and picked up the object Bess had seen, which was draped over the back.

My yellow-and-white-striped T-shirt.

Which had been packed securely in my luggage.

"Is it really yours?" Bess called, as I examined the shirt. I checked the tag: yes, right size. And really, what were the chances of someone else—in *Costa Rica*—having the exact same shirt I'd bought at a small boutique in River Heights two or three years earlier?

"It's definitely mine," I replied, looking back at Bess. She looked just as confused as I felt.

I turned to the right, peering into the dense foliage to see if I could spot any other clothes. At first I didn't see anything unusual, but then it jumped out at me: a light blue piece of fabric, tucked under a huge green plant with large, shiny leaves. I moved closer and grabbed the cloth: It was the top half of Bess's bikini. And this one actually had Bess's initials inked onto the tag.

"Oh my gosh!" Bess cried, watching me. "It looks like someone dragged it through the mud!"

And it did. But I had a feeling that—and the dirt that was streaked over my T-shirt—was more the result of spending the night in a rain forest than anything else. Before getting back on the trail, I searched the area some more and found two socks, an unfamiliar pair of shorts, a ruffly blouse, and a bottle of contact lens solution.

"This is definitely all from our group's luggage," I told Bess as I got back onto the trail, carrying my shirt and her bikini top. "But how on earth would it get here?"

Bess shrugged. "Well, one thing's for sure. It was no accident." She looked at her watch. "It's taken us forty minutes to walk from the lobby to this point on the trail. Somebody brought our stuff here very deliberately!"

I nodded. "And it would have to be someone familiar with the resort," I added. "I mean, to even know to hide it here."

Bess sighed, fingering her bikini top with a sad expression. "I got this sixty percent off!" she complained. "It's a Lucky Ricci, you know."

I nodded, having no idea what she was talking about, but fairly sure it was some kind of hoity-toity designer. Bess shops like some people train for marathons. And she's frighteningly good at it.

"We'd better get back," I said, glancing at my watch. "It's only half an hour till dinner. And I'm sure everyone will want to know about what we found."

"Yeah," Bess said with a sigh. "Though I'm sure they'll be sad to know most of our luggage is probably gonzo."

It was a sad, quiet hike back to the main building. It took us a while too—we didn't pass the sign with the maps until ten minutes after dinner started.

"Gosh, I feel bad," Bess murmured, looking at the time. "Enrique's been preparing us such amazing meals, and we're late."

"Let's hurry," I suggested, catching a whiff of something that smelled like a spicy beef stew. "My stomach just remembered how hungry I am."

We doubled our pace, speeding through the gardens and hurriedly throwing open the back door of the inn.

Once inside, Bess and I glanced at each other and frowned. Were our watches wrong? Because if they were right, our group should have been midway through dinner, laughing and talking in the dining room. Instead we were met by uncomfortable silence.

Finally Deirdre's strident voice cut through the quiet. "Well, so far, this vacation is turning out to be anything but!"

I met Bess's eye, and we both ran into the dining room. Inside, our group was all huddled around a couple of seats at the table, and their dinners were sitting untouched on their plates. Juliana stood off to the side, holding a pitcher of water and looking troubled. I almost didn't see Cristobal at first, but soon realized that he was standing behind her, a stricken look on his face.

Everyone seemed to be looking at something in Frankie's hand. In fact, Frankie and Sarene seemed to be at the center of the group, looking down at whatever Frankie held.

"This is no minor annoyance, Deirdre," Frankie was saying. She waved whatever she was holding in the air—it looked like a piece of notepaper. "This isn't like when Cristobal lost our luggage. This is a threat!"

I glanced over at Cristobal. He looked horrified—and just as confused as my friends.

"What's a threat?" Bess asked, and everyone turned to face us.

"Wow, Nance," said George, suddenly popping up

from the rear of the crowd. "*You* definitely have to see this!"

She grabbed the paper from Frankie, who looked less than thrilled about giving it up. Then George ran over to Bess and me and pressed the note into my hands.

I looked down. It was in fact notepaper, with a piece of tape still attached to the top.

"This was taped on Frankie and Sarene's door when they went to change for dinner," George explained.

I looked down. A message was written in huge block letters.

TELL YOUR <u>NEW YORK GLOBE</u> THAT
CASA VERDE IS A SHAM. LOOK DEEPER.
AND WATCH OUT!

"Oh my gosh," I whispered, turning to look at Cristobal. "What's going on here?"

FRANKIE AND NORA

Cristobal tried to laugh, but it came out kind of strangled. I could tell by the look in his eyes that he was just as thrown by the note as we were. "Well . . . ," he said finally. "Well."

I didn't want to add to his distress, but I knew I had to tell him about what Bess and I had seen. "There's more," I spoke up. He met my eyes, looking concerned. "Bess and I just went for a hike on the Coco Trail. After about forty minutes, you cross a bridge over a little stream."

Cristobal nodded. "I know the bridge," he said. "Is there a problem?"

Bess broke in. "Well, the *problem* isn't with the

bridge so much as . . . what we found near the bridge."

Cristobal frowned, looking confused now. "Which is?"

Bess held up her muddy bikini top. "This!"

"And this," I added, pulling my striped T-shirt out of my back pocket, where I'd stuffed the end. Everyone gasped, taking in the muddy clothing.

"Our clothes," Bess explained.

Cristobal looked from Bess's top to my shirt, back and forth, like he couldn't make sense of what he was seeing. "Your clothes?" he asked, furrowing his eyebrows. "But *por qué* . . ." He sighed, seeming to remember that the eleven of us were still watching him. "Why on earth would your clothing end up there? This must be unrelated—perhaps these belong to Alicia or Sara, the veterinary staff."

"We met Sara yesterday," I said, "but there's no way these belong to her. I'm telling you, I recognize my shirt. And Bess is sure this is her top. There were other things strewn in the mud too—contact lens solution and a ruffly purple blouse."

Poppy gasped. "That's mine!" she cried. "I got it through work, straight from the designer. It's very expensive!"

Adam sighed, turning to his girlfriend. "I told you not to bring it on this trip," he said. "In these developing countries, who knows what they do with the luggage?"

Poppy glared at him. "Our luggage was completely safe," she said, leveling her glare at Cristobal, "until we got here!"

Cristobal was staring blankly out the window, as though his brain was desperately trying—and failing—to make sense of this new information. After a few seconds of silence from the rest of us, he seemed to realize that we were waiting for a response. He jumped a little, pasting a smile on his face as he looked from one unhappy guest to another. "I am so sorry," he said, his eyes warming sincerely. "I think— perhaps—this is someone's idea of a prank? Someone's very, very bad idea." He laughed nervously, but no one joined him. "My children," he went on, "are very young—seven and nine. They live with me, here, on the grounds. Perhaps they are feeling jealous of *Papá's* attention to the guests, and this is their way of getting some for themselves. In any case, don't worry. Casa Verde will, of course, pay to replace everything." He swallowed hard, probably tallying up the costs in his head. Who knew what kind of designer duds Poppy had brought? Not to mention Bess and her super shopping skills.

"Thank goodness I didn't bring my laptop," George whispered to me, sidling up on my right.

Frankie, however, was pouting. "What about the things that are irreplaceable?" she asked. "I had a bookmark signed by the late John Updike."

Sarene nodded. "Or a little packet of my best reviews, that I carry everywhere."

George sighed, and I glanced her way. "Like that's a surprise," she whispered, shaking her head at Sarene.

Cristobal cleared his throat. "Tonight," he said, "I will enlist Enrique's help, and we will go down to the stream. We will salvage everything we can and bring it back here, for you to inspect in the morning. Then, later that evening, we will go shopping in San José so that you can replace as much as possible. What cannot be replaced, we will reimburse you for."

Frankie snorted. "Fat chance of that. Can you bring John Updike back to life?" Frowning, she elbowed Sarene and gestured to the note. "I've had enough socializing for today. Let's bring that up to our room and see if we have any insights." She glanced briefly in the direction of her fellow guests. "Good night, all." And just like that, she and Sarene had disappeared up the stairway to their room.

We all looked back at Cristobal, who looked beyond crushed.

"Ohhh, Cristobal," Hildy cooed, immediately going into "mom" mode. "Don't you worry about this little setback. I can promise you that as long as our belongings are replaced, *I*"—and here she flashed a hard look at Poppy—"won't write about this unusual happening. I'm sure that whoever's behind it, it's an innocent mistake."

Poppy stared blankly for a few seconds before adding, "Sure, me too."

Adam scoffed. "Are you *serious*?"

We all turned to look at Adam, but he was staring accusingly at Poppy.

"I understand that you want to help this guy out, and hey, free vacation, but if I paid to come here and then found out his little rugrats scattered my clothes all over the rain forest, *I* would not be so understanding."

Poppy just looked at him for a moment before responding, very slowly, "I guess it's a good thing you're not the journalist, then."

Adam looked stunned—then furious. He looked angrily over at the rest of us, then jumped up from his chair. "That's it. I'm tired and I'm going upstairs. Good night."

"Good night," we all echoed, and Cristobal reached out to grab Adam's elbow.

"Sincerely, sir," Cristobal said, in an almost pleading tone. "I am very sorry this happened. I will make it right."

Adam looked into Cristobal's eyes for only a

moment before pulling his elbow away. "You'd better," he said simply, and then disappeared up the stairs.

When he left, it was quiet for a moment. I think we were all tired—physically, from the jet lag, and emotionally, from everything we'd seen that day.

"Well," Cristobal said finally, "I'd better get Enrique and begin collecting your things. We will bring a snack up to your rooms. Good night, friends."

"Good night," we replied.

Cristobal stalked through the dining room and into the kitchen, where we could hear him unleashing a torrent of upset-sounding Spanish at his brother. Enrique replied something, and then Cristobal cut him off, raising his voice. Soon it sounded like the two were engaged in a good old-fashioned family fight.

I elbowed Bess and George. "That doesn't sound like a man who's convinced this is the work of some harmless prankster."

Bess nodded, looking thoughtful. "I'm beginning to think there's more going on at this little family-owned resort than meets the eye."

The next morning I woke with a feeling of purpose. Everything seemed much more manageable after a good night's sleep. Sure, this whole losing-all-our-belongings thing, as well as the threatening-note thing, was upsetting. But I was Nancy Drew! I'd gotten to the bottom of much more dangerous things before. Step one: Wrangle the threatening note from Frankie.

"Oh, *hi,* Frankie," I greeted the *Globe* reporter with a huge smile, leaning casually against a table in the hallway outside their room.

Frankie looked at me blankly. "Hello, Nora," she replied, then hoisted her purse on her shoulder, about to breeze past me.

"Actually," I said, reaching out to touch Frankie's shoulder, "it's *Nancy.* And I was wondering: Might I trouble you to borrow the note you got last night?"

Frankie came to a full stop now, turning around to face me. "What would *you* want with that?"

"I'd just like to have a look at it," I clarified. "You know, give it a little look-see. Maybe I can figure out where it came from."

Frankie snorted. (She did that a lot, I was realizing.) "You think *you* can figure out where it came from?" she asked. "You're a teenager. I'm an investigative journalist. You do the math."

She whirled around, ready to stalk off again, but again, I reached out and grabbed her shoulder. *"Actually—,"* I began.

She turned around, annoyed now. "Actually?"

"Actually, I know quite a lot about investigations,"

I said, smiling toothily. "It's kind of a . . . hobby of mine."

Frankie sighed. "Look, I watched *Veronica Mars* too," she said. "It was a great show. Very entertaining. But *fictional*."

She was totally losing me here. I decided to get right to the point. "Can I have the note?"

She snarled, "What will you *do* with it?"

"Just examine it!" I held up my hands in a gesture of surrender. "I just want to have some time to look at it—maybe notice some details you missed! Then I'll give it back."

Frankie continued to stare at me, now looking more curious than angry. It seemed to completely flummox her that I wouldn't just give up and go away. I could see the confusion in her eyes: Who *was* this crazy teenager? And why wouldn't she go back to her friends and stop bothering her?

Frankie took a deep breath, her eyes never leaving mine. "All right," she said slowly, reaching into her purse. "I've already made a color scan and sent it back to the office for our handwriting analysts to look at."

I looked up at her. "You have a computer here? That wasn't lost with your luggage?"

Frankie rolled her eyes. "Only a total *amateur* of a writer would surrender her laptop," she said with a sigh. She reached into her purse, pulling out a laptop no bigger than a discount paperback. "This is my baby," she told me, then put it back and pulled out another tiny device. "And this is my portable printer/ scanner. Both absolutely priceless—to a journalist who's worth her salt."

"Wow," I said. "My friend George is kind of a technophile—I think it's killing her to be away from a computer for so long. Do you think maybe she could borrow yours to check her e-mail?"

Any friendliness in Frankie's eyes suddenly evaporated. "Absolutely not. You think I'm going to hand over my priceless baby so you can gunk it up with puppy videos and Jonas Brothers screen savers? Fat chance."

Okay, then. "Well, listen. I'll take very good care of this. And I'll give it back to you this afternoon, okay?" *After I make a copy.*

Frankie nodded, looking at me with—could it be?—a tiny glimmer of respect. "Let me know what you see, kid," she said, hoisting her purse back onto her shoulder and turning to leave. "Maybe we can work together."

Hmm, I thought, watching her ramrod-straight posture as the stalked away from me, nose in the air. *Maybe. Or maybe not.*

• • •

"Well," Cristobal greeted all of us about an hour later, as we were finishing up breakfast in the dining room. Juliana wove around the big table, taking away empty glasses and dishes. She caught her uncle's eye and smiled. He winked, and she disappeared into the kitchen.

"Enrique and I scoured the preserve land last night," Cristobal went on. "We were attacked by spiders. We were harassed by monkeys. But ultimately," he paused, gesturing behind him into the lobby, "we came back with many usable items."

Everyone at the table jumped up, with Poppy taking the lead as we all ran into the lobby. "Oh my gosh!" Poppy cried, grabbing the purple ruffled blouse and a gold high-heeled sandal. "My things! And they're clean!"

Enrique nodded. "Juliana helped us," he explained. "Last night the three of us stayed up late, cleaning everything." He paused as we all moved closer, searching the lobby's sitting area for familiar items. "Anything that must be dry-cleaned, of course, we will pay for."

I glanced over at Bess and George, who were excitedly gathering some shirts, shorts, and socks.

"Look, Nance," Bess called, happily picking up a blue sweater and throwing it my way. "They found one of your cardigans!"

"Great," I responded, reaching down to pick up a few things myself. All in all, two of my shirts and one pair of jeans had been salvaged. The rest of my belongings, I assumed, had been beyond repair.

"If you can take your things upstairs," Cristobal announced, "we'll get on the bus and be on our way to La Paz Waterfall Gardens!"

"Ooh, waterfalls," George cooed, in a very un-George-like tone. "Good thing they found my camera!"

"There's still something fishy about this," I told her quietly, glancing sideways at Cristobal. "I feel like there's something he's not telling us."

George looked from me to our guide. "Maybe," she allowed, "but if they're replacing our things, what does it matter?"

I took Frankie's note out of my pocket. "And what about this?" I asked, unfolding it for George.

George's eyes widened. "How'd you get your hands on that?"

I sighed. "I think I kind of agreed to work with Frankie," I admitted. "Or something. Either way, I've got to get to the bottom of this. The person who left the note must be the same person who stole the luggage, right?"

"One more thing," Cristobal said, holding up his hand to stop the flow of traffic out of the lobby. He suddenly turned very serious. "After speaking to my family, I realize that I must apologize to you all. My children, who as I told you, are a bit unhappy about how much attention this resort has been getting, thought it would be funny to steal your luggage. They took it out to the hiking trails, and the animals must have gotten to it from there."

I frowned. "Animals were able to open our suitcases?" I asked.

Cristobal cringed.

"And your seven- and nine-year-old kids were able to drag twenty-three suitcases forty minutes into the rain forest?" I pressed on.

Cristobal sighed again. "I do not know the details," he said simply. "I know only that they confessed. And I am sorry. And I will replace your lost items."

"What about this?" a shrill voice piped up from the right, and I turned to see Frankie, holding up a scanned printout of the note I still had in my hand. "Did your kids leave this note, too? 'Look deeper'?"

Cristobal nodded, looking uncomfortable. "They did."

Frankie raised her eyebrows. "How did they come up with this wording, then?" she asked. "This doesn't sound like a child at all."

Cristobal shrugged, looking frustrated now. "Who can tell where children get their ideas?" he asked.

"Perhaps they saw it on television. Or read about it in a book. I don't know. I know only that I will do whatever I can to make it right."

Frankie looked unimpressed. I could tell that she, like me, was sure there was more going on than what Cristobal was telling us. She looked my way, catching my eye with a *Can you believe this?* expression. I shrugged, holding up the note so she could see it, and then put it back in my pocket. *I'm working on it.*

An hour or so later I sat squeezed next to Bess in Casa Verde's cozy minibus, studying the note on my lap. "The handwriting's pretty hard to read," I observed, tracing the large letters with my fingers. "Block letters. Hard to tell if it's a male or female. It's almost like they were trying to write in as nondescript a way as possible."

Bess glanced down and yawned. "Right," she agreed. "I don't know what you're going to get from that, Nance."

I fingered the edges of the note, sighing. I *wasn't* getting all that much useful information. And a small, petty part of me worried about returning the note to Frankie Gundersen and admitting that I'd found nothing. More than likely, that would convince her that I really was a silly teenager—and keep her from sharing information in the future.

"Wait," I said, suddenly noticing a tiny raised area along the top of the note. It was barely visible—just a couple of dots and the bottom of an arc, in green ink, whereas the note had been written in black. "Do you see that?"

Bess looked. "Hmm," she said, fingering the top edge of the note where I was pointing. "Oh, yeah. It's like—"

"A doodle?" I supplied, bringing the note closer to my face. "A kind of code, maybe?"

Bess reached over and pulled the note out of my hands, taking a good look herself. "I don't think so." She frowned at the paper, then handed it to me while she retrieved her huge, overstuffed purse from the floor and began digging in it. "Here!" She pulled out a brochure and showed it to me: GET UP CLOSE AND PERSONAL WITH NATURE AT CASA VERDE.

"Sold!" I said, glancing sideways at Bess with a smile. "Though I think that brochure leaves out the part where they strew your luggage all over the muddy rain forest floor."

"No, not that," Bess insisted, directing my attention away from the text. "*That.*"

She was pointing to the logo next to Casa Verde's name: a brilliant sun, with a delicate-leafed plant growing up along the side. I looked from the logo to the note in my hands, and sure enough, the bottom of the sun and the plant matched up perfectly with the tiny marks at the top of the note.

"It's the logo," I realized.

"Right," said Bess. "It looks to me like someone wrote this on resort stationery. They tried to cut the logo off, but . . ."

"They didn't get it all," I supplied, staring at the note. *LOOK DEEPER. AND WATCH OUT! I* shuddered. "So if they wrote it on hotel stationery . . . and if all our luggage was ditched deep in the resort's nature preserve . . ."

"Then it looks like someone from the resort must be responsible," Bess finished, looking a little concerned herself. "But who?"

I sighed. "That's the million-dollar question." Who at Casa Verde would want its guests to "look deeper"? And why? Was someone on staff getting shortchanged in some way?

Before I could think too much more about it, we arrived at La Paz Waterfall Gardens. Cristobal climbed out and immediately took on his "tour guide" persona.

"All right ladies and gentleman!" he greeted us. "Welcome to one of the most beautiful spots in Costa Rica! Here we'll see several waterfalls, along with bountiful wildlife: frogs, butterflies, birds, orchids, snakes . . ."

"Snakes?" Kat piped up, a little nervously. She was just getting off the bus, with Pretty Boy—who was now dressed in the "Funky Safari" outfit that Cristobal had salvaged from the preserve—sleeping in her arms. "Pretty Boy is a little freaked out by snakes."

Cristobal looked from Kat to the tiny golden bundle in her arms. "Ahhh," he said, not sounding happy. "You brought Pretty Boy."

Kat slid her oversize sunglasses from the top of her head down over her eyes and rubbed Pretty Boy's head. "I *always* bring Pretty Boy. He's my other half."

"Hmm," said Cristobal. "Excuse me for a moment."

As our guide darted off toward the ticket booth, Pedro, the driver, helped the rest of the reporters off the bus and offered us sports bottles filled with water from a portable cooler.

"Listen," Robin whispered, looking around with an enchanted look on her face. "Can you hear them?"

I listened. Sure enough, there it was: the soothing, crashing sound of falling water. We must be very close to the waterfalls. "Wow," I said, giving Robin a little wink. "Have you ever seen a waterfall before?"

"Never," she replied. "And I can't wait to see the frogs, too!"

Cristobal returned with an odd look on his face— he looked concerned and relieved at the same time. "Kat," he said, "I am so sorry, but dogs are not allowed in the park. There is concern that Pretty Boy might hurt some of the local wildlife."

Kat pushed back her sunglasses again, revealing furious eyes. "Pretty Boy isn't just a *dog*," she stressed. "He's a *companion*."

"Still." Cristobal shrugged, grabbing a bottle of water and gesturing to Pedro to pack up the cooler. "I think it is best that he stay here with Pedro."

Pedro looked from Kat to Cristobal, looking notably unexcited about this new development. *Sorry*, I spotted Cristobal mouthing to his employee. But Kat was too beside herself to notice.

"I'm *never* separated from Pretty Boy!" she cried. *"Never!"*

Deirdre, who was holding a bottle of water and looking eager to get into the park, touched her cousin's elbow. "Kat," she said gently, "maybe it *is* for the best."

Kat pouted. "Oh, *Dee,*" she huffed. Right then, it was very clear that these two were related. Kat had every ounce of Deirdre's tenacity—and the same focus on herself. But after a few moments of sulking, Kat sighed deeply and walked over to Pedro, theatrically placing Pretty Boy in his arms. "He likes his belly rubbed," she said, sniffling. "And whatever you do, *don't* take off his outfit. Pretty Boy is very uncomfortable without his dog clothes."

Pedro looked from Kat to the dog in his arms, not seeming to know what to make of that statement.

"Thanks, Pedro," said Cristobal, with a sincere smile to the driver. "We'll be back in a couple hours. Now, my friends . . ." He turned to face us, holding out his arms to encompass our whole surroundings. "Prepare to be dazzled by nature!"

Dazzling was definitely the word for it. Along with *stunning, breathtaking,* and *unbelievably beautiful.* Walking along the trails of the park, I often felt like I'd somehow been transported inside a touristy postcard. The sky was just too blue, the waterfalls too powerful. How had I managed to find such a beautiful place?

"This is what my heaven looks like," George breathed as we took in the last amazing waterfall. "Gorgeous scenery, abundant wildlife. And knowing that this land will be protected from development."

I nodded. "It's really like paradise."

We'd been through another butterfly garden, the frog exhibit, and several nature trails. After the waterfall, we stopped to eat a leisurely picnic lunch before getting back on the bus.

"Aren't you glad we came here?" Deirdre asked her cousin, nudging her with the end of a fork. "Even though Pretty Boy had to stay on the bus?"

Kat was silent for a second, but then she nodded and

a slow smile spread over her face. "It *is* amazing," she allowed. "I just wish Pretty Boy could have seen it."

George turned to Deirdre, who looked sincerely happy as she sipped her water and popped a piece of watermelon into her mouth. "Deirdre," she said, "doesn't seeing places like this make you want to do everything you can to protect the earth? I mean, beyond just what you see celebrities do?"

Deirdre cut her eyes at George, and for a moment I tensed, ready for her to attack. But just as quickly, her face relaxed and she shrugged. "I guess I am seeing how little things make a difference," she admitted. "Like with these water bottles," she added, tapping hers. "Normally I would just buy a bottle of water and throw it out when I was done. But this water tastes just as good, and with these reusable, biodegradable bottles, I can use them over and over without making any new waste."

Cristobal, who was sitting a few seats down, overheard her and smiled. "I'm happy to hear you say that," he said. "I know that your vacation has not gone completely smoothly so far, but really, that is what we want to do at Casa Verde: show you how beautiful the environment can be, while teaching you how to care for it."

Satisfied, we packed up our plates and silverware and headed out to the parking lot.

"Pedro!" Cristobal called, playfully patting Kat's arm. "Pedro! Quickly! Tell us that Pretty Boy is okay! Kat has been worried sick!"

There was no response from our bus, and Cristobal chuckled quietly. "He is angry at me," he whispered to George and me. "I don't think Pedro likes the small dogs."

George grinned. She was no fan of "the small dogs" either, so I wondered if she was planning to sympathize with Pedro. As we got closer to the bus, though, there was no sound from within. No calls from Pedro—and no barks from Pretty Boy, which was *really* odd.

"Pretty Boy?" Kat called, starting to sound a little nervous. "Sweetie pie, where are you hiding? Did you miss Mommy?"

Now we were rounding the back of the bus. Running up to the door, Cristobal peered inside and gasped. He ran through the open door before any of the rest of us could see what he was so upset about.

I glanced at George, and we ran to the door. Inside, Cristobal was gently slapping a slumped-over Pedro, who was draped over the steering wheel, out cold.

"Oh my gosh," I breathed. I ran onto the bus, glancing down the aisle. "Is he okay? Is Pretty Boy here?"

"Maybe he is just asleep," Cristobal replied with a

nervous laugh. "Pedro! Pedro?" But I could hear the concern in his voice.

Turning back to the seats, I walked down the aisle, looking left and right. "Pretty Boy? Pretty Boy?" I called. Within seconds, I could hear Kat stepping onto the bus, joining my calls: "Pretty Boy! *Pretty Boy!*"

In the last row, I saw it. "Oh, no," I groaned, hesitantly reaching out to grab it.

"He's *drugged*," I heard Sarene crying in disbelief from the front of the bus. "Someone drugged our driver!"

"Oh my God!" Kat squealed as she saw the object in my hand. It was Pretty Boy's "Funky Safari" outfit—with no Pretty Boy inside. Instead, when I picked up the tiny jacket, a note fell out.

I DON'T THINK YOU'RE LISTENING TO ME. THIS IS SERIOUS. IF YOU REALLY LOVE ANIMALS, STAY AWAY FROM CASA VERDE. I'LL HOLD ON TO YOUR DOG UNTIL YOU LOOK DEEPER.

YOUNG HOOLIGANS

"**W**hat does that mean? Look deeper?" Deirdre cried as Kat began to hyper-ventilate. Deirdre glared at Cristobal. "Is there some dark secret about Casa Verde that you're not telling us?"

Cristobal looked pained. "No," he said, and from his body language, I thought he seemed sincere. "I—I have no secrets."

"Well, it seems like it's gone beyond a harmless prank," Frankie observed, glancing up from the note, which she'd taken immediate possession of. I was trying to get a good look from over her shoulder, and she was more or less humoring me. "So far we've had our luggage stolen, a dog kidnapped, a driver drugged, and two threatening notes. What's next?"

"We have to get Pedro to a doctor," George urged, looking down at our still mostly unconscious driver. He was beginning to respond to his name with moans, and to move around a little, but he was still nowhere near alert. "We don't know what he was drugged with. What if it's dangerous?"

"No!" Kat shrieked, bursting into sobs. "We can't leave without Pretty Boy! What if he's right nearby?"

George looked to Cristobal, who still seemed unsure of what to do. He stared into nothing, eyebrows furrowed, looking confused. Suddenly a new look of determination flashed in his eyes, and he stood up from his crouching position. "No. We must go back to Casa Verde."

"Go *back*?" Hildy asked. She had settled onto a seat in the van, and she held a frightened-looking Robin in her lap, stroking her hair. "But Cristobal, a crime has been committed here! What if Pedro is in danger?"

Cristobal set his jaw. "This is no crime," he said with certainty. "A dangerous prank, yes. But I know who is behind this, not to worry. And I have a full-time nurse on staff at Casa Verde who can check on Pedro. I am sure he will be all right, though. See?"

He reached out and held the side of Pedro's face, and Pedro moaned at the touch. "He is coming out of it. He just needs time."

I sighed, staring at the note in Frankie's hand. THIS IS SERIOUS . . . LOOK DEEPER . . .

Frankie turned subtly and murmured to me, "This is getting shadier by the second."

I looked up at Cristobal, who was securing Pedro for the ride. "I will drive!" he announced, in an almost challenging tone. I wanted to believe Cristobal was trustworthy and that everything at Casa Verde would be fine—but it was getting harder and harder to believe that.

"Agreed," I whispered to Frankie.

"We'll talk back at the resort," Frankie said in a low voice, barely moving her lips. Then she made a big show of sighing and turning to Sarene. "I guess we should take our seats, then."

Kat was still crying, though. Her sobs had gone from hysterical to tired and heartbroken. "But Pretty Boy!" she whimpered. "What if he—?"

"We will find your dog," Cristobal said coolly. He had settled himself in the driver's seat and was already starting the bus. "Don't you worry."

But I could see that Kat *was* worried—very worried. And while I wasn't one of Pretty Boy's number one fans—like Bess, I'd gotten my share of nips while trying to be friendly—I felt terrible for her. It must be hard to lose a beloved pet in a strange country, and to have no idea how to find him.

Slowly everyone settled back into their seats. Deirdre wrapped her arms around a still-crying Kat and tried to comfort her. It didn't take long for Cristobal to get the bus moving, and soon we were on our way home.

Frankie, who was sitting up front with Sarene, finally turned impatiently to Cristobal. "Do you think it was someone who works for you?" she asked.

"What?" Cristobal asked, although he had to have heard her.

"The person who kidnapped Pretty Boy," Frankie clarified. "The person who drugged your driver! It would almost have to be someone who works at the resort, don't you agree?"

Cristobal stared ahead at the road. Still, I could see a dark look on his face. "Let's not talk of sad things now," he said. "Didn't you enjoy the waterfalls?"

Adam, who was sitting in the second row with his arm lazily wrapped around Poppy, snorted. "Yeah, we enjoyed them a lot," he said forcefully, "*until we got back to the bus and found our driver unconscious and a dog missing.* That kind of put a damper on things!"

"Adam," Poppy cautioned, giving him a *cut it out*

look. Adam just sighed deeply and looked out the window.

"Yes, it was upsetting," said Cristobal. "But what can you do? Young hooligans these days, they're capable of anything."

"So a young hooligan did this?" Frankie pressed, leaning forward.

Cristobal pressed his lips tight, seeming to realize what he'd just accidentally let slip. "I shall say no more until we know for sure," he said. "But rest assured, we will get to the bottom of this. Now, if you look to your right, you'll see a sugar cane plantation. . . ."

I watched Cristobal, amazed, as he shifted effort-lessly back into "tour guide" mode. How could he be so calm? And did he really know who was behind the attacks?

As I was about to give up my analysis and grab a quick nap on the way home, I noticed Frankie looking in my direction. She widened her eyes, raising her eyebrows. Her expression seemed to ask, *Are you as freaked out by all this as I am?*

I nodded, shrugging my shoulders. *Yes,* I thought. *But I really* am *going to get to the bottom of this—no matter what it takes.*

"Cristobal," I called, running from the lobby back to the driveway, "can I help you, please?"

We'd just arrived back at Casa Verde, and my fellow tourists were distracted by a snack, which had been put out in the dining room. They milled around, telling Juliana and Enrique what had happened, but just as I'd started to get settled, I'd realized that Cristobal was still out here with Pedro. And if his earlier behavior was any indication, he was probably going to try to get Pedro to the nurse—if there really was a nurse—before anyone could see.

He looked up, and for a second, a flash of annoyance lit in his eyes. But he quickly pasted on his normal friendly smile. "No, thank you, Nancy, I can handle this on my own. Enjoy the food my brother prepared. I will let you know what I find out."

He gently led Pedro, who was conscious now, but still groggy, out of the bus. Pedro squinted in the bright sunlight and moaned.

"Mi cabeza," he said. *"Muy dolorosa. Tengo hambre."*

I wasn't sure what he was saying, but I knew I wanted to be there for the rest of it.

I ran over to the two men, pasting on a cheery smile of my own. "Oh, don't be silly," I insisted. "Enrique made such an amazing lunch, I don't think I'll be hungry again for weeks. And I don't mind helping at all. It will only take a few minutes, right?"

Cristobal turned to me, his expression ambivalent. He sighed, finally, and nodded quickly. "Right," he said in a resigned tone. "Just a few minutes."

Pedro was already leaning on his boss, but I put my arm around him from the other side so we could both support his weight. Cristobal led us around the main building to the side facing the pool, where I now noticed a small Red Cross sign posted on a white door. He knocked once, twice, and then stood back while a smiling older woman answered the door.

"*Buenas tardes,*" she said. "*Ah, Senor Arrojo! Puedo ayudarle?*" Then she seemed to notice Pedro and me for the first time. Glancing at me, she abruptly switched to English. "My goodness!" she cried. "Pedro! What happened to you?"

"*No sé,*" murmured Pedro, walking into the small office and sitting down on the examining table.

"Violeta, Pedro drove us to La Paz Waterfall Gardens this morning," Cristobal explained. His eyes flashed toward me. "While we were touring the grounds, there was an . . . incident. When we came back, we found Pedro in the bus, unconscious."

Cristobal stopped there, so I piped up, "And one of the guests' pets was missing. And there was a threatening note—something about looking deeper at Casa Verde?"

Violeta's eyes widened in alarm, but she looked just as surprised by this as we all had felt. "Someone took your dog and drugged Pedro? *Dios mio!* How could such a thing happen?" She turned to Cristobal, looking for answers.

Cristobal shrugged, glancing at me. "I, ah . . . I have my suspicions," he replied. "But right now the important thing is to make sure Pedro is okay. I would like to know what he was given."

Violeta nodded. "Of course, of course." She began buzzing around Pedro, checking his vital signs, and then asked him a bunch of simple questions, like what day it was and what his full name was.

"Hmm," she said finally. "Well, Mr. Arrojo, I think Pedro will be fine. I won't know for sure until we do blood tests, but my guess is he was slipped some sort of tranquilizer. If I am right, he'll be groggy for a while, but eventually he'll get back to normal."

Cristobal nodded, looking thoughtful. "And a tranquilizer . . . anyone could have access to that?"

Violeta shrugged. "It's hard to say. Some are widely available, some are not. We'll have to wait and see which one he was given."

As Violeta prepared to take Pedro's blood and Cristobal seemed to think this over, I spoke up. "Pedro," I said. *"Habla inglés?"*

Pedro looked at me a bit woozily but nodded. *"Un poco."* I didn't know much Spanish, but I knew from my own pathetic attempts to speak it that *un poco* meant "a little." Pedro and I were on the same level:

I spoke *un poco* Spanish, he spoke *un poco* English.

"Did you drink water—*agua*—from a bottle while you were on the bus?"

Pedro nodded. *"Sí. La droga está en el agua."*

He'd lost me at *sí*, but I pressed on. "And the bottle of water—was there any way to tell it was yours?"

Pedro nodded again. *"Sí,"* he said, gesturing, as though he were showing me the top of his bottle. "My name," he explained. "I write on top."

I glanced at Cristobal. "And were the bottles kept here?" I asked. "Would anyone have been able to get to your bottle before we left?"

Cristobal frowned, seeming to get where I was going. "Of course. The water bottles were filled last night, so they would be cold for our trip."

"Right," I said, flashing a grateful smile at Pedro. "So—it seems like the drug was probably put into Pedro's bottle here. Don't you think?"

Cristobal sighed. He stretched, turning away from me, toward the door. "I suppose it's *possible*," he replied. "Listen, Nancy, why don't you let me get to the bottom of this?"

I ignored his question. "And if someone drugged Pedro's bottle here—that's pretty serious, don't you think?" I asked. "He was our *driver*. We were lucky that he didn't drink any water before we were parked, but what if he'd been drinking on the drive there? What if he'd lost consciousness at the wheel? We could all have been seriously injured in an accident."

Cristobal took a deep, slow breath. "I know you are concerned," he said. "But Nancy, we will get to the bottom of these pranks. And I believe they are pranks. Sometimes kids do things that are more dangerous than they imagined."

"So you're still saying your kids are behind this?" I asked, stunned. What kind of monster kids did Cristobal have, who had access to tranquilizers and pet-nappers? Or, more likely, was he just trying to make me stop asking questions?

"Nancy," Cristobal said soothingly, though he still wouldn't meet my eye. "You are on vacation, and you are a young girl. Please, let me handle this. Relax. There is no conspiracy here."

He paused; in the quiet, we could hear Juliana calling the guests down for dinner.

"Nancy," he coaxed, "go eat, please. In the morning, this will all seem like a silly misunderstanding."

I fought the urge to contradict him, and flashed a quick smile at Violeta and Pedro as I backed out of the nurse's office and headed back to the dining room.

One thing was for sure, though. I didn't think there was anything *silly* about any of this.

MRS. ARROJO

In the dining room, everyone was clustered around Kat, who was still crying on Deirdre's shoulder. It had been hours now since Pretty Boy went missing, but I didn't think Kat had stopped sobbing. When I walked in, Bess and George caught my eye and quietly made their way over to me, as the rest of the group kept trying to comfort Kat.

"What happened?" Bess whispered, walking up to me with a grave expression.

I sighed. "Well, it looks like Pedro was given some sort of tranquilizer," I explained, "but they won't know what exactly until the results from his blood test come back tomorrow."

George frowned. "Will he be okay?"

I nodded. "He's much better now—just a little groggy. Violeta, the nurse, said that the drugs should wear off completely by tomorrow morning."

Bess took in a deep breath. "Well," she said finally.

"Well," I agreed.

"It's pretty freaky, right?" she went on. "How do you think it was given to him?"

I looked over at our group, where little Robin was offering Kat one of her stuffed animals. "All of our water bottles were filled and left in the hotel fridge overnight. Pedro's was labeled. So it makes the most sense that someone put the tranquilizer in his water while it was in the fridge."

George looked concerned. "Then they followed us to the park and hid out in the parking lot, waiting for Pedro to pass out so they could swoop in and grab Pretty Boy."

I nodded. "I think so."

"So, the water being drugged here would seem to imply it was someone from the hotel," Bess suggested.

"Right," I agreed. "That, and the note we looked at this morning." I paused. "Speaking of which—who has the note that was left in Pretty Boy's outfit?"

George smirked. "Who do you think?"

"Frankie?" I asked.

"Righto." George gestured over her shoulder, where Frankie, who was standing behind the crowd trying to comfort Kat, was squinting at the note in her hand.

I let out a breath. "Well," I said, "I'd like to get a better look at that. Here goes nothing."

I walked up to Frankie, trying to paste a helpful smile on my face. "Hey," I greeted her. "Find anything?"

Frankie glanced up from the note to me, looking less than thrilled. "Nothing much," she admitted, "but I'm about to scan it and send it to the *Globe* to see what they can figure out."

"Hmm," I murmured. "Did they get back to you about the last note?"

Frankie nodded. "Of course."

"So?" I prodded. "What did they find out?"

She sighed, looking like she wasn't too happy about this. "Not much," she informed me. "Since the person used block letters, there wasn't much to analyze. They said based on the pressure used on the pen, it was probably a female, but that was far from certain."

I nodded. *That doesn't sound terribly helpful.* "Anything else?"

"Well, based on the person's tendency not to close up his or her letters, they're probably unsatisfied with their life," Frankie explained.

"Huh," I murmured, not sure what to say. It was sounding like the *New York Globe*'s state-of-the-art analysis wasn't going to help us solve this mystery. Which wasn't exactly a surprise—but it did, somehow, make Frankie's sense of superiority a little more frustrating.

I paused, unsure what to do. I could share everything we'd learned with Frankie—about the first note being written on hotel stationery, and thus probably by an employee or guest, and about what I'd learned from Pedro. I could enlist Frankie as a partner, and we could try to solve this thing together.

But something stopped me from opening my mouth. I had a terrible feeling that there was no such thing as a "partner" for Frankie—*especially* not a teenager. If I told her what I knew, I sensed that I would end up trailing along after her whims and ideas, more of an assistant than anything else.

And I just wasn't sure the case would get solved that way.

"Well," I said finally, pulling the first note, the one left on Frankie's door, out of my pocket. "I looked this over, but, umm . . . you know."

Frankie glanced at me curiously, then her eyes widened in understanding. "I know," she said. "Not much to go on, right?"

"Right," I agreed, relieved I hadn't had to lie. "Um,

can I see the new note? Just for a second?"

Frankie nodded easily and handed it to me. It was small and square—just about the same size as the first. And even though the culprit had written in block letters again, it was easy to tell that the same person had written both. I fingered the paper, comparing it to the first note. I could tell, just from the weight and texture, that the newer note had been written on the same stationery—Casa Verde's stationery. So, another note from within the hotel.

After a moment, I looked up at Frankie and shrugged, smiling gamely. "Oh, well. I'm not getting much, but thanks."

"No problem," said Frankie, taking back both notes. "Don't worry—I'll keep on it."

Before I could respond, Enrique and Juliana emerged from the kitchen. Enrique carried a plate of vegetables and dip, and Juliana held bottles of wine and water, ready to serve all of us guests. "Dinner is ready!" Juliana announced in her cheery voice, and we all began milling toward our seats. At her place at the table, Kat dabbed at her eyes with a (recycled) tissue and tried to pull herself together for the meal.

Enrique quickly set down the veggies and dip in the middle of the table, then pulled off a smaller plate that I hadn't noticed. He approached Kat, his eyes warm with sympathy.

"Señorita Kat," he said gently, "I understand you lost someone special today. I brought you a little piece of flan. Sometimes sweet flavors can soothe the heart, no?"

Kat looked up at him, her eyes watering. "Oh, Enrique, that's so kind."

He placed the flan in front of her. "Please, enjoy."

Just then we heard loud footsteps from the entrance, leading us all to turn to the lobby. There stood a beautiful middle-aged woman, with long, curly black hair that fell midway down her back. She had round, expressive brown eyes, lined with lots of black eyeliner, and she wore pale pink lipstick. She was dressed formally, in a blazer and dark pants, with a cheery pink scarf knotted around her neck.

She glanced at us awkwardly, then called back into the offices: "Cristobal! *Mi amor!*"

Within seconds, Cristobal emerged from his office and ran to this woman like they were starring in *Gone with the Wind*. They kissed, and then the woman let loose a torrent of Spanish, and Cristobal responded, his rapid speech making it impossible to follow with my *poquito* understanding of the language. Helplessly I turned to Bess.

She glanced at me, then back at the couple. "She says she missed him all day," she said, understanding instinctively that I wanted a translation. Bess, who'd taken Spanish in high school, was much better at the language than I was. "She had a hard day at work, something about an old tree that didn't want to be moved. And he's saying . . ." She paused. "Her name is Virginia, and he says he needs to tell her something, and let's go to the office."

George watched the couple disappear into Cristobal's office. "That must be his wife."

I nodded. "And I'll bet he's going to tell her what happened with Pedro and the notes."

"Right," said Bess, turning back to the table and taking a sip of the water Juliana had recently poured us. "I'll bet."

I turned back to the table, but then glanced up, confused by something on the periphery of my vision. There, in the middle of the dining room, Enrique was standing stock-still as he stared into the lobby. His hands were empty, since he'd already dropped off the vegetable tray and Kat's flan, and his hands were balled into fists. When I looked at his face, I gasped: He looked completely heartbroken. His eyes were glued to the spot where Cristobal and Virginia had disappeared, and his mouth hung open.

Before I could nudge Bess or George, Juliana suddenly seemed to notice her father, and she ran to his side, her eyes filled with dismay. *"Papá!"* she cried, getting up close to him and putting her hands on his shoulders. Slowly he pulled his eyes away from the lobby, and Juliana began speaking to him in Spanish—so quietly that I couldn't make out a single word. She turned him toward the kitchen, then, rubbing his back comfortingly, seemed to guide him back there. Just before they disappeared, Juliana turned to face the rest of us, a bright smile pasted on her suddenly much-older-looking face. "I'll be right back! I want to hear all about what you saw at La Paz."

"Did you see that?" I whispered to Bess and George when they left.

"See what?" asked George. "The smooch in the lobby? We were all just talking about that."

I shook my head. "No, I—" I paused. I realized I didn't want anyone else in our group overhearing me, for fear of embarrassing Enrique, who'd been so sweet to us. "I'll tell you later," I whispered to my friends, turning my attention to our meal.

Maybe it was just a spacey moment on Enrique's part. Maybe he'd been thinking about something totally unrelated, like a sick relative or a dreaded chore. Maybe his heartbroken expression had nothing to do with his brother and his wife, or what was happening to his guests at Casa Verde.

Maybe. But I was going to have to do a bit of sleuthing tonight to make sure.

A LITTLE NIGHT SNOOPING

That night I lay awake in my bed long after the inn grew quiet around me. Soon Bess and George's breathing slowed, and I knew they were fast asleep. I waited an hour or two more, reading with a flashlight to occupy myself, just to make sure that no one would be up and about. Then I put down my book and flashlight, tossed off the covers, and threw on a pair of dark jeans and a black hoodie sweatshirt that George had bought with her luggage replacement money.

I knew I could have told my friends about my plans to snoop that night, but I figured it would be easier to get information alone—and besides, I really didn't know what I was looking for. It just felt like *something* was going on between the Arrojo brothers that I didn't fully understand yet. Neither one of them seemed like a criminal to me, and I couldn't figure out what either brother stood to gain by sabotaging his own business, trying to frighten guests. Still, both threatening notes contained that mysterious phrase, LOOK DEEPER—meaning that whoever was leaving them thought they knew a deep, dark secret.

And who was more likely to know a deep dark secret than one of the people in charge?

Moving as quietly as I could, I shoved my flashlight in my pocket and slowly, silently, opened the door to our room and slipped out. The lights in the hallway were off, but the huge windows at either end of the hall let in lots of moonlight. I was able to easily find my way to the stairway and then tiptoe down into the lobby.

I knew where I was headed: Cristobal's office. A little part of me felt guilty for sneaking around, trying to gather information on the man who had been so hospitable and warm to us. And the funny thing was, despite his strange behavior today, I still felt pretty sure that Cristobal didn't have anything to do with the notes. But I *did* believe that he knew more than he was letting on. And I'd given him ample opportunity to come clean to me, but he'd made it clear that in his opinion, this was none of my business.

In my world, though, everything's my business—especially when someone is getting hurt.

I snuck through the lobby and down the hallway to Cristobal's office. Around me, the building was so quiet that I could make out the leaves rustling outside. I thought of Kat suddenly, and hoped she was getting some rest after the awful day she'd had. If my investigations went as I hoped, maybe she'd be getting Pretty Boy back soon.

Cristobal's office door was closed, and when I carefully tried to push it open, I realized it was locked. Not a huge surprise—especially after the way Cristobal had been acting today. Fishing in my pocket, I pulled out my battered ATM card. It's jimmied so many locks for me over the years, it's amazing that it still works to take out cash, too.

I slid the card between the door and the jamb, carefully sliding down to where the lock engaged. I could tell that this was just a simple lock—nothing fancy like a computerized system or a deadbolt. It would be easy to pick.

Click! "And voilà," I whispered to myself, smiling. I twisted the knob and gently pushed the door open.

Inside, the office was small and neatly organized, with two filing cabinets, a desk with a blotter, a fairly new computer, and an appointment calendar. My fingers itched to turn on the overhead light, but I knew it was probably too risky. Instead I clicked on Cristobal's small desk light—bright enough to help me see, but not so bright that it would alert anyone outside the office to my presence.

With the light on, I noticed a small stack of papers on the desk. Probably invoices and communications that hadn't been filed yet. Either that, or these were papers that Cristobal had taken out to examine in light of everything that had happened today. I jumped on them eagerly.

Bills, bills, and more bills. I flipped through invoices for what my limited Spanish revealed to be furniture, organic vegetables and meat, and cleaning supplies. To my dismay, none of this seemed all that exciting—or in any way related to what had happened to Pretty Boy. I examined each invoice, frowning, wondering what I was missing. At the bottom were a bunch of papers on stationery from Green Solutions—a company that, I noticed, was headquartered in a suburb of Chicago, back in the United States. This bill was in English.

Thank you for selecting Green Solutions for all your eco-needs. Enclosed is an itemized invoice detailing all the renovations we've contracted for Casa Verde. As you can see, we have completely overhauled your electric, plumbing, and heating/cooling systems. All are now completely environmentally responsible and feature brand-new, state-of-the art equipment. . . .

I bit my lip, flipping through the attached invoice. Low-flow showers . . . gas-powered stove . . . bamboo blinds . . . It all seemed pretty reasonable. So Cristobal and Enrique hadn't renovated the resort to make it totally green themselves; they'd hired an outside consultant. That made sense and, I imagined, was probably pretty common. If it was hard enough for Deirdre to figure out that her cute koala bear tote bag was actually the antithesis of green, imagine how hard it must be to make a whole resort eco-friendly! Consultants to help you navigate through the world of green products were probably more than helpful; I bet they were necessary.

Unfortunately, though, the papers weren't getting me any closer to a solution. I dropped the stack back on the desk and decided to try the filing cabinet behind me—which, to my delight, was unlocked. Flipping through the files, I found one called Finances and quickly pulled it out. Maybe Cristobal or Enrique had some shady expenses they didn't want getting out to the public . . . maybe the dognapper had dirt on them?

A few minutes later, though, all I'd learned about

Casa Verde's finances was that they seemed to be perfectly in order. The brothers had indeed split the expense of buying and renovating the resort, each putting up 50 percent of the start-up costs. Sliding the Finances folder back into the cabinet, I smiled as I noticed some childlike drawings tacked up on the wall. One showed a big house, with stick figures for "Mama," "Papá," "Maria," and "Felipe"—and a whole zoo's worth of animals behind them. "CASA VERDE!" was written at the top of the drawing. I smiled. *That doesn't look like a picture drawn by a hooligan,* I reflected, remembering Cristobal's claim that his children had somehow stolen our luggage.

I looked around the room, searching for other drawings or photos. On the far corner of the desk, I found one. In the center of the large photo—eight by ten or so—stood a tuxedoed Cristobal and a beautifully made-up Virginia, wearing a poufy, old-fashioned bridal gown. Her hair was teased high, eighties style, and a rhinestone tiara sat on the top of her head. Around them stood what I assumed were family members—two older couples, and a few smiling men and women that I assumed were siblings. *Wait!* I thought, looking closer. *Where's Enrique?*

I searched every face in the photo but didn't recognize the kindly cook. Was it possible that he hadn't attended his own brother's wedding?

And if so, why not?

I frowned, trying to figure it out. Maybe I was making something out of nothing—maybe Enrique had simply felt under the weather on his brother's wedding day. But then I remembered the awful look on Enrique's face as he'd watched Cristobal and Virginia embrace. Could it be related?

Sighing, I sat down on Cristobal's desk chair to rest for a moment. It was getting late, and I had to get up early the next morning to check on Pedro's blood test results. I didn't quite trust Cristobal to tell me the truth, and I wanted to get the news from Violeta directly, at the same time he did. I was beginning to feel tired. Should I just go back to bed? As much as I wanted to get closer to finding the dognapper, I didn't seem to be getting much useful information. . . .

Wait. Suddenly I spotted something on the left side of the desk blotter. The golden light from the small desk lamp barely illuminated the whole desk, casting the left side in shadow. And there, I realized, was a set of indentations on the desk blotter. Big block letters, as though someone had handwritten something on the desk, and the pressure had left an indentation on the blotter below.

Oh my gosh. I grabbed a piece of paper from the printer that sat under the desk. Looking around frantically, I spotted a mug of pens and pencils near the computer and quickly grabbed a pencil. Placing the paper over the indentation, I very, very carefully slid the side of the pencil lead over and over the paper. Slowly, very slowly, the letters formed by the indentations dropped out of the rubbing, becoming clear: CASA VERDE IS A SHAM. LOOK DEEPER.

I shuddered. *Oh, no.*

The threatening notes—left by the same person who'd ruined our luggage and stolen Kat's beloved pet—had been written right here!

Were we in danger? Was it possible that Cristobal had snowed us all, convincing us that he was a warm, cheerful entrepreneur—when in fact he had darker motives?

But *why*? Why would he hurt his own business?

"Ay, Papá, cálmate . . ."

I jumped, my heart thumping hard in my chest. The words were very loud—and very close. Someone was just feet away from the door to Cristobal's office, and from the sound of things, they were headed my way!

LATE-NIGHT SECRETS

Acting on instinct, I dove under Cristobal's desk just as someone pushed his office door open.

"Hmm," I heard a voice say. *Enrique!* "That's strange. Cristobal forgot to lock his office."

"*Ay, Papá—*"

"Juliana," Enrique interrupted his daughter, "speak English, please. We agreed you would practice your English at the resort."

Juliana sighed deeply. "Okay, Dad!" she said with fake cheerfulness. "As I was saying, he was probably so excited to see Virginia—"

"*Ay, mija!*" Enrique exclaimed, breaking his own rule.

"—he was probably *sooo* thrilled to see the love of his life, he forgot what he was doing!"

I frowned. Juliana's tone was angry and sarcastic— I'd never heard her sound like that. Up to now, she'd easily been the sunniest personality at Casa Verde. She was able to come and go as she pleased, leaving the resort for school every day, and coming in for only a few hours to help her father.

"Well," Enrique said after a moment, sounding as though he were making an effort not to sound angry, "if that is the case, it's none of our business." He stepped into the office and began walking around, to the shelves, to Cristobal's desk, to the filing cabinet. . . . I sucked in my breath, hoping like crazy that I hadn't left anything out that would alert him to my presence.

"Isn't it?" asked Juliana, a little petulantly. "What are you looking for, anyway?"

"A letter I got today," Enrique replied. "An invoice from Green Solutions. Ah, here it is." I heard him pluck a paper off the desk, then fold it and shove it into his pocket. "I worked with them more closely than Cristobal, so I wanted to look it over. Are you ready to go?"

"I've been ready for hours," Juliana said.

I heard Enrique walk back toward his daughter. "I'm sorry, *mija*. Tomorrow's *ropa vieja* just meant a lot of cutting and prep work. With all the excitement today, I didn't get started on it until this evening."

Juliana sighed. "I know. It's no problem. I was napping in my study room."

Enrique's voice softened. "Ready, then?"

"Really? Are we not going to talk about it?" Juliana's voice was filled with concern.

"Talk about what?" said Enrique. "*Mija*, you worry too much."

"Come on, *Papá*." It sounded like Juliana was standing by the door. "Every time you see her, you're in a terrible mood for hours."

My ears pricked up. *Her?*

"That's not true." I heard Enrique take a couple of steps toward the door, but he stopped when Juliana began talking again.

"Why can't you admit it? You're angry at him, and you're even angrier at her. And you have every right to be!"

Almost unconsciously, I leaned closer to Enrique and Juliana, as though by getting closer I could begin to understand this conversation. *Angry at him? Even angrier at her?* Were they still talking about Cristobal and Virginia? And if so . . . did this have anything to do with Enrique not attending his own brother's wedding?

Enrique sighed deeply. "This conversation is

finished. Let's go home, Juliana. You're tired."

Juliana sighed. *"Papá . . . ,"* she protested

"This conversation is finished!"

Even in my spot under the desk, I jumped at the sudden rise in Enrique's voice. It was especially startling because he was usually so soft-spoken, even shy. I never would have expected him to yell at his daughter like that! Clearly, what she had said to him really hit a nerve.

I heard him stomp out of Cristobal's office, and then I heard his heavy footsteps trail down the hallway and out to the lobby. Juliana stood still for a moment.

Perhaps this was an old argument.

"Juliana?" From the lobby, I heard Enrique call his daughter, his voice back to his normal, gentle tones. "Come on. We're both tired. Let's go home."

"Yes, *Papá,*" she called. She waited another moment or two, then turned and walked out to meet her father.

I took a deep breath. Then, slowly, I unfolded myself from beneath the desk, still clutching the rubbing I'd made of Cristobal's desk blotter.

You're angry at him. She must have meant that Enrique was angry at his brother. I remembered Enrique's sudden heartbroken look at dinner that night—just as Virginia walked in. I remembered

Juliana gently leading her father back to the kitchen.

You're even angrier at her. And you have every right to be.

What had Cristobal and Virginia done to make Enrique so angry?

And how did it relate to the scary notes written in this very office?

HORSING AROUND

The next morning I was exhausted and wanted to sleep in more than anything, but I forced myself out of bed and into the shower so I could visit Violeta before breakfast.

"You're up early," George observed, sitting on her bed and watching the bathroom door when I emerged, "for someone who was involved in some sort of late-night shenanigans."

I froze. "What do you mean?" I asked. I really had no problem with Bess and George knowing about my snooping last night—in fact, I had planned to tell them as soon as we had a private moment together—but George's knowing tone made me wonder if I'd clumsily let the whole group in on my adventures.

"Come on, Nance," Bess said sleepily, sitting up from her bed and running her hands through her hair with a yawn. "You may be stealthy, but George and I have known you for a long time. We heard you sneak back into the room around, say, one a.m.?"

I looked from Bess to George, relieved. "Why didn't you just ask me then?" I asked.

George shrugged. "We had a pretty good idea what you were up to," she explained. "I saw your eyes bug out of your head at dinner last night when Enrique saw Cristobal and Virginia."

I gulped. "Was I that obvious?"

Bess laughed. "Only to people familiar with your mannerisms," she assured me. "Don't worry. Everyone else probably just thought you had heartburn."

I snorted. "Great!" Walking over to my bed, I dumped my pajamas on my pillow and quickly grabbed my things. "I'll tell you everything on the bus today, I swear," I promised. At dinner the night before, Cristobal had told us that due to the stress of the day, he was going to postpone our planned wildlife cruise and take us on a relaxing beach day with horseback riding this afternoon. Breakfast was at eight, and we would be boarding the bus to head out at nine. "But right now, I need to head down to the nurse's office and see whether Pedro's blood tests came back."

"Sure," Bess joked, shaking her head with mock annoyance. "You're keeping secrets, Nancy Drew, and don't think George and I are going to let you get away with it!"

"Oh, I don't," I promised Bess, dashing past her and George on my way out of our room. "Remember, I've known you two a long time too."

It looked like Violeta had just gotten to her office when I arrived, breathless from running, at her door. She glanced up at me curiously, then carefully placed her purse on a chair by her desk and walked over to the door to flip over the NURSE IS IN! sign. "Hello, miss," she greeted me, a little warily. "Forgive me, but I don't remember your name."

"It's Nancy," I said, trying to smile warmly, although I knew it was clear from my panting that I'd raced here and was in some kind of hurry. "I was just wondering if you'd gotten Pedro's blood tests back yet."

Violeta looked thoughtful, as though trying to remember, and then shook her head. "Oh, no," she replied. "It takes twenty-four hours. I should have them later today, though."

I nodded. Shoving a hand into my purse, I grabbed a receipt and a pen. "My name is Nancy Drew and I'm staying in room six," I explained, writing both pieces of information on the back of the receipt.

"Can you please leave me a copy of the test results when they come in? You can just shove it under my door. No need to bother Cristobal."

Violeta looked at me, her expression unsure. "You are very concerned with the results?" she asked.

I nodded. "Violeta," I said, "has anything like this happened at Casa Verde before? Threatening notes, things missing?"

Violeta shook her head. "Oh, no. But of course, you are our first guests."

I frowned. Of course she was right. Casa Verde hadn't really been open long enough to have much of a history.

"Has there," I began, and then paused, trying to decide the best way to phrase this. "Cristobal and Enrique—they seem very close as brothers, right? I mean, are they close?"

Violeta looked a little surprised by my question, and not entirely pleased. "Of course," she said, turning away from me to walk back to her chair. "They bought this resort together, no? Now, is there anything else I can do for you?"

She turned back to me, her eyes hard and impatient. She didn't look angry, exactly—just finished with this conversation and eager for me to leave her office. *Wow*, I thought. *Was I really obnoxious there, or is Violeta hiding something about her employers?*

"Nothing," I admitted, flashing a smile again. "If you could just give me those results when you have them, I'd appreciate it."

Violeta nodded, relief in her eyes. "Sí. Enjoy your day, miss."

"Nancy," I reminded her, but she had already turned back to her desk, and she ignored me.

"So," I whispered to George and Bess, hunkered down in the rear corner of the Casa Verde bus. Cristobal was driving, giving Pedro another day to recover, but he still kept up a running commentary on the sights we were passing—which kept most of our fellow group members distracted. "You saw the look Enrique had when he saw Cristobal and Virginia, right?"

George nodded. "I honestly might have missed it, if I hadn't seen your eyes bug out."

"Yeah," Bess agreed. "We could practically see the detective part of your brain go into overdrive!"

I grinned. "Well, last night I decided to do some snooping in Cristobal's office. I just feel like there's a lot he's not telling us—and I wanted to get to the bottom of it."

George nodded. "And?" she asked, at the same time a new face popped up over her shoulder.

"What's this about getting to the bottom of things?" Frankie hissed, looking from me to George to Bess, her eyes filled with suspicion. "You're not keeping anything from me, are you? I thought we were working on this together."

George and Bess both looked from Frankie's accusatory face to my blank one, their eyes widening in sympathy. What to do, what to do? I bit my lip, unsure. Maybe, if I shared everything I knew, Frankie could help me, but . . .

Could I trust her?

"No," I assured her, shaking my head. "It's just, well . . ." I sighed. Maybe I was being silly, trying to keep everything to myself. I might as well come clean. Two heads were better than one . . . right?

Of course, that all depended on which two heads you were talking about.

"I noticed some tension between Cristobal and Enrique at dinner last night," I said finally. "So I decided to check things out last night after everyone had gone to bed. I broke into Cristobal's office—"

Frankie's eyes widened to the size of dinner plates. "You *broke into* Cristobal's office?!" she hissed. "Listen, Nancy, investigation is not some kind of pretend game."

"She knows," Bess and George chorused.

Frankie looked at them in surprise.

"She knows," Bess repeated.

"Trust us," George said in a bored tone. "Nancy knows all about the dangers of sleuthing."

Frankie looked from them to me. "Okay," she said slowly. "So let's assume you totally safely and responsibly broke into Cristobal's office." She paused, excitement lighting up her fine features. "What did you find?"

"Well," I said, trying to remember what I had and hadn't told Bess and George. "For one thing, the threatening notes have all been written in Cristobal's office."

Frankie's mouth dropped open. "How do you know?"

I shrugged, like these sorts of discoveries were no big deal for me—which, by the way, they aren't. "I did a rubbing of his desk blotter," I replied. "And there were all kinds of phrases from the notes—in the same handwriting."

Frankie looked impressed. "Wow. So it must be a hotel employee!"

I shook my head. Actually, I didn't like the degree of certainty in her voice. "Well, it means it was written by someone who has access to Cristobal's office. Which means either an employee, a family member, or a close friend."

"Or a guest," suggested Frankie, looking thoughtful.

"Maybe," Bess agreed, examining her finger-nails. "But only if they had Nancy's mad break-in skillz."

George grimaced. "Was that 'skillz' with a *z*?" she asked her cousin.

Bess nodded nonchalantly. "You know it."

"*Anyway,*" I said, trying to get back on track. "That's not all I found out. While I was in Cristobal's office, Juliana and Enrique came in. They were having an argument."

Frankie gasped. "Did they see you?"

"No." I shook my head. "I ducked under Cristobal's desk."

Frankie nodded, looking a little surprised. "Well—what did they say?"

I sighed. "It seems like there's something going on between Cristobal, Enrique, and Cristobal's wife, Virginia. Juliana said something about Enrique being mad at Cristobal, and even madder at Virginia . . . and having every right to be."

Frankie looked thoughtful. "Wow. Maybe . . . maybe it's business-related?"

I shrugged. "I'm not sure. According to all the documents I found, they own Casa Verde fifty-fifty. It seems like it would be in their best interest to work things out."

Bess nodded. "Unless it's personal," she suggested. "Personal slights between family members can be hard to let go of."

"That's true," allowed Frankie, with a faraway look.

"I can probably still remember every harsh thing my sister ever said to me."

George looked like she understood. "Nobody can hurt you like your family can."

We were all quiet for a minute, thinking this over.

"Well," Frankie said finally. "This is good info, actually. Thanks, Nancy, for sharing it with me."

I tried to smile. The truth was, I wasn't totally sure whether telling Frankie had been a good idea. I guessed I'd find out soon.

"When we get back to the resort," added Frankie, turning to go back to her seat toward the front of the bus, "we can try to put this information into action."

With those words, she walked away, and I nodded weakly. *Put this information into action.* I wasn't so sure we were ready for action yet. As a sleuth, I've learned that only bad can come from jumping the gun on your suspicions . . . and something about Frankie put me on edge.

The beach that Cristobal took us to, near a town called Quepos, was unbelievably gorgeous. A wide swath of white sand gave way to perfectly turquoise water, and in the background, multiple trails wound through a lush rain forest. Our entire group laid out towels on the sand and spent the morning and early afternoon reading, napping in the sun, or splashing in the cool blue waves. It was exactly the sort of relaxing day we all needed after the drama of yesterday.

Of course, Pretty Boy was still missing, and Kat still looked miserable 90 percent of the time. She lay quietly on the beach blanket she shared with Deirdre, barely speaking, not at all like her usual bubbly self. But whereas yesterday she had been crying nonstop, today she was subdued. "I still can't believe he's gone," she said softly when Bess asked her how she was holding up. "I just hope that wherever he is, he's happy."

At two o'clock the serenity of the beach was suddenly disrupted by the sound of hoofbeats. We all looked up—and saw Cristobal and a couple of young men leading a trail of horses onto the beach!

"All right, everybody, look alive," Cristobal announced with a smile. "You didn't really think I would let you lie around and mope all day, did you? Now that you've relaxed, let's take a horseback ride so you can see some of the natural beauty of the rain forest."

We all glanced at one another. Robin, who had been pushing sand into a big pile to make a sand castle, beamed at the horses. "Oh my gosh! *Real* horses!" she shouted, jumping up and running over to them.

Hildy laughed, dropping the magazine she'd been reading onto the sand. "She *loves* horses," she told Cristobal with a smile. "How did you know?"

Cristobal shrugged. "Call it intuition." He laughed. "Remember, I have a daughter too."

Robin's enthusiasm seemed to be all we needed to warm up to horseback riding. Soon we were all climbing aboard horses, helped by the young men who, Cristobal explained, rented him the horses from their stable down the road. "These horses are very gentle, very well trained," he explained, as one of the young men smiled with pride. "My family and I have used them many times. The horses are calm and friendly enough to carry even young children. They've been walking this trail for years, and they know it as well as they know their own stalls."

I had been assigned to a fawn-colored mare named Mariposa, who regarded me with warm brown eyes as I reached out to pat her nose.

"She is very serious, very elegant, no?" asked the young man who was helping me mount her. "You will have no problems with her. Mariposa will take good care of you."

"Uh-oh," I heard from George behind me, who

was reluctantly climbing up on a brown mare named Isabella. "She's moving. Is it normal for her to move like that?"

"She is a living animal, señorita," her helper replied, gently patting George's leg. "She is very gentle, though. You'll be fine."

"Don't worry, George," Bess called from the horse behind her. "Blanca and I will look out for you. If we see Isabella getting out of line, Blanca will *neigh* really loud!"

George looked unconvinced. She gripped the reins and a hank of Isabella's mane nervously. "Do horses even neigh here?" she asked.

"Oh, come on, you guys," called Deirdre, who was turning around on her horse a couple of places in front of us with a disapproving look. "Grow up!"

I looked up and noticed that Kat, who was on the horse in front of Deirdre's, was smiling back at us.

"Lighten up, Deirdre," Bess replied with a smile. "We're on vacation."

"Are we ready?" asked Cristobal from the lead horse, calling our little skirmish-in-the-making to a halt. "Is everyone comfortable on their horse? Shall we head off?"

Poppy clutched at her reins, looking a little wobbly. "I'm not sure," she said nervously. She was on one of the largest horses, a black gelding named Juan.

"Oh, come on, Pops," said Adam impatiently, reaching out to steady her. "We know all these horses are very calm. Just relax and let's go."

Cristobal cocked an eyebrow at the squabbling couple, as if waiting for them to finish. "Shall we go?" he asked again.

"Let's go," Hildy said. She and Robin were settled on a couple of chestnut mares and looked eager to begin our tour. Robin bounced up and down on her horse, stroking its ears, looking thrilled to be atop her favorite animal.

"Okay," Cristobal agreed. He urged his horse forward, and all of our horses followed obediently without us having to do a thing. Cristobal had been right when he said these horses were very well-trained! They followed along like they'd been treading this path their entire lives—which they probably had.

"Wow," breathed George as we made our way through the jungle. "This is actually really relaxing."

"It's a cool way to see the jungle, too," Bess added.

We rode along the narrow but well-trod path, and Cristobal pointed out different plants and animals. It never ceased to amaze me how abundant the wildlife was in Costa Rica. Again, we saw monkeys, tropical birds, even a few white-tailed deer. And the rain forest itself was so colorful and rich. "I could get lost in here," I said with a sigh as we crossed a narrow wooden bridge over a stream.

Suddenly a harsh, shrieking sound cut through the calming sounds of the rain forest. I looked ahead and realized that the horrible shriek was coming from Cristobal's horse!

"Cálmate! Cálmate!" Cristobal was urging the animal as it reared up on two legs. He desperately grabbed the reins and even a piece of the horse's mane, but they seemed to slide like silk through his hands. Before any of us fully understood what was happening, Cristobal was falling to the ground, and his horse was running away through the forest.

Kat's horse, which was right behind Cristobal, was clearly spooked by the other horse's fear. She, too, let out a screeching sound and reared up on her back legs. Soon all the horses were spooking in a chain reaction, though the people in the front clearly had the worst of it.

"Calm down! Calm down!" I begged Mariposa as she tensed and backed up, hoping she wouldn't buck me off. She snorted, clearly perturbed, but kept all four feet on the ground.

In front of me, everyone was still recovering from the scare. I could see that Kat and Deirdre had managed to get their horses back on all fours, but they were still pacing anxiously, and the girls were struggling to control them. Cristobal was trying to call to his horse, who still capered through the forest, clearly not ready to resume the tour.

"What happened?" I called, pulling on the reins to bring Mariposa to a complete stop. "What spooked your horse, Cristobal?"

I climbed off Mariposa as gracefully as I could (which was not very gracefully) and dropped to the ground. Then I ran over to where Cristobal was standing and Deirdre and Kat were struggling to calm their horses. Cristobal was still calling to his horse in the forest, making gentle, calming sounds, but when he saw me coming he ran back to the path where his horse had spooked.

"Ah, I am not sure," he said quickly, sliding into my path. "It could be anything. Perhaps a bird taking flight, or a monkey moving too quickly."

"But you said these horses were trained!" Sarene called from the back of the line, where she and Frankie were bringing up the rear of our group. "If they're used to walking through the rain forest, why would a little wildlife cause your horse to freak out?"

Cristobal shrugged, looking uncomfortable. "Ah," he said, "perhaps it was a noise. Or a reflection of the sunlight in the stream. You know, even the tamest of animals can be unpredictable."

Speaking of reflection, I caught sight of something small and shiny on the path over Cristobal's shoulder. I moved forward, clearly not about to let him stop me. "What's this?"

"What?" asked Cristobal, moving quickly in reverse. He reached down to pick something off the path, but I moved too fast for him to get to it first. In a snap, I was around him and diving down to grab the shiny object I'd seen. It look me a minute to figure out what I was holding.

"What the . . . ?" I muttered, looking down at a small toy fire truck.

"Oh, what is it?" Cristobal suddenly asked, moving quickly to my side. He reached out his hand as if to grab the toy from me, but I jerked away, not ready to give it up yet. "A little toy! Look at that! Some child must have left it behind, and the reflection of the light shining off it must have spooked my horse. . . ."

"I don't think so," I said, turning the toy over in my hands.

Someone had taped a note to the truck's underside.

"What's going on?" Frankie demanded from right behind me, then came around to get a look at the truck. She must have dismounted her horse also— no doubt she was as curious about this incident as I was.

"It's a note," I said, holding the truck out so she could see. Together we read the now familiar block letters.

LOOK DEEPER, OR IT GETS WORSE.
I DON'T WANT TO HURT ANYONE.
BUT I WILL.

I gasped.

There was a moment of silence before Frankie murmured, "We're lucky no one got hurt today. Someone obviously meant to spook our horses and cause some kind of accident."

Pulling the note off, I noticed a small switch on the truck's plastic bottom. Gently I pushed it, and jumped as the toy suddenly started vibrating and beeping. The lights on the top of the truck illuminated, flashing bright red. The whole effect was probably more than enough to freak out even the most well-trained horse.

"That's how they did it," Frankie murmured. "Press the switch, leave the truck in the horse's path."

I looked at Cristobal. "Looks like our little friend has struck again," I said insistently. Why hadn't he wanted me to see this truck? What was he trying to hide?

He just looked at me with a resigned expression,

then sighed and turned back off the path, calling to his horse again.

LOOK DEEPER.

I gulped. What was the writer of these notes trying to make us see?

THE WRONG PARTNER

"I'm sorry. I just don't have much of an appetite," Kat said softly as Juliana took away her still-full plate of fruit and pastries. When we'd returned to Casa Verde, Cristobal had run into the kitchen and convinced Enrique to whip us up an amazing snack to soothe our nerves. The pastries and fruits were delicious, but sadly, they didn't seem to be doing the job. All of us were sitting around the table with our heads on our hands, looking as frightened and upset as we felt.

"I'm so sorry about what happened today," said Juliana gently, looking from one face to another. "I hope you all know, my uncle and my dad are doing everything they can to figure out who's behind this."

Are they? I wondered, biting my lip. Cristobal had always seemed truly upset by these notes, and by what had happened to our group, but then why was he acting so strangely today, trying to hide the real cause of the incident from us? I hated to think that he was somehow involved in ruining his own press tour, but it was beginning to feel more and more likely. What had happened between him and Enrique? Was one of them trying to ruin the press tour, and along with it, the chances for Casa Verde's success?

"Oh my gosh!" I said suddenly, jumping up as a thought occurred to me. When Bess looked at me like I'd lost my mind, I explained, "Pedro's blood test results! They're probably ready by now. I asked Violeta to leave me a note, but I haven't been up to the room."

"What's that?" I hadn't even heard Frankie get up from her seat, but suddenly she was there behind me, her voice sharp and impatient. "Blood test results? Well, let's go see Violeta together!"

Oops. I looked at Bess and George, and I'm sure my regret showed on my face. I hadn't meant to announce where I was going to Frankie. Now she was surely going to join me, and I was going to lose control of my own investigation.

Bess and George looked sympathetic, but they

didn't seem to know what to do. "Well . . . good luck, Nance," George told me, taking a sip of Casa Verde's very own coffee. "Let us know what you find out right away."

Frankie tapped my shoulder, more impatient than ever. "Let's go, Nancy," she commanded. "I have some questions for this so-called *nurse.*"

I nodded and tried to stifle my sigh as I followed Frankie to the door leading to the nurse's office. *Poor Violeta won't know what hit her.*

"*Sí,* I have the results," Violeta said after we had appeared in her doorway and Frankie had asked her gruffly where the blood test results for Pedro were. "Didn't you get my note?" She gave me a sharp *Why are you bringing this rude woman to interrogate me?* look.

"I didn't," I said, trying to sound as apologetic as I felt, "but I haven't been back to my room. We went horseback riding today, see, and there was . . . another strange incident."

Something seemed to spark in Violeta's eyes, and she turned to me curiously. "Another incident?"

"Someone tried to spook our horses with a loud, flashing toy and cause an accident that could have hurt lots of people," Frankie told her, in a somewhat accusatory tone. "Do you know anything about that?"

Violeta looked stunned. "No," she said simply. "That's awful. Was anyone hurt?"

"No," I replied, trying to look friendlier than Frankie—which wasn't hard. "It was just upsetting, as I'm sure you understand."

Violeta nodded. Her eyes gave away nothing. "Of course."

"Anyway," Frankie said with an impatient sigh, "the results?"

Violeta frowned at her, then turned and plucked a piece of paper off her desk. "Ah, yes. As it turns out, Pedro was given a drug that caused him to pass out."

"Yes?" Frankie said shortly. "And that drug was?"

"Midazolam," Violeta replied, as though that explained everything. When she looked up and noticed our blank faces, she went on, "It's an animal tranquilizer."

An animal tranquilizer? I shuddered. That sounded dangerous. "Will he be all right?" I asked.

Violeta nodded, looking sympathetic. "He has been through the worst of it. It's mostly out of his system now. He may feel a bit groggy today, but he should be fine."

I glanced at Frankie. She looked dubious, as though this information left her with a whole new set of questions.

"An *animal* tranquilizer?" she asked Violeta, as

though she didn't completely believe her. "It's never used on humans? It's not something, for example, you'd find in a *nurse's office*?"

I cut Frankie a sharp look. I had no idea why she was being accusatory with Violeta, of all people—unless she simply didn't know how to ask questions in any other way.

But Violeta didn't seem offended. If anything, she seemed amused by Frankie. "No," she said. "It is used only on animals, because it can give humans headaches and cause memory loss."

"Is it well known?" I asked, taking over for Frankie. "Is it something you would ever come across if you weren't a veterinarian?"

Violeta looked thoughtful. "Not really," she replied.

"Do you need a veterinary license to get it?" I asked.

Violeta nodded. "Oh, yes."

I frowned. That left out all the Arrojos, and most of the Casa Verde employees. "Could it have been used to drug Pretty Boy as well?" I asked, as the thought suddenly occurred to me. "I mean, to keep him quiet while he was being dognapped?"

Violeta seemed to consider this. "Sure," she said after a moment. "If the person knew the right amount to give him."

Frankie tapped her lips with the tip of her finger. "So this came from a veterinary office," she said, "or someone *stole* it from a veterinary office." She glanced at me, and I shrugged. I wasn't ready to make those assumptions yet.

"Is it fast acting?" I asked Violeta, still trying to get a handle on what had happened to Pedro.

"Oh, yes," she said, nodding. "It puts animals to sleep right away. Vets sometimes use it to make treating difficult pets easier. If you have a dog that's violent or very frightened, for example, you can give them some midazolam and treat them while they sleep."

I met Frankie's eye. "If it's fast acting," I said, "then someone must have put it in Pedro's water bottle, and we were just lucky that he didn't take a sip from it until he was parked."

Frankie's eyes sparked with recognition. "He could have taken a drink at the wheel," she realized, "and then we could have been in an accident."

I nodded. "Whoever did this doesn't care if innocent people get hurt," I said ominously.

Violeta looked stunned. "Surely . . . ," she said, "surely it's a mistake, no? Who would want to hurt you, or Cristobal, so badly?"

Frankie's eyes widened suddenly, and she turned to me and grabbed my arm. "Come on, Nancy," she said. "Thanks, Violeta. I think Nancy and I need to question someone else now."

Violeta stared after us, still looking surprised, as Frankie pulled me out of her office.

"The veterinarians," Frankie said simply, dragging me along the path through the gardens and down toward the nature preserve.

"The—the veterinarians?" I repeated, struggling to keep up. Frankie had turned into a woman on a mission. She was walking so briskly and strongly, I was pretty sure that if a tank pulled into her path, she'd simply walk over it to get to where she needed to go.

"There's a nature preserve, right?" Frankie asked impatiently. "And if I'm not mistaken, when Juliana gave us the whole spiel at dinner the first night, she said there were two veterinarians on staff to look after the animals on resort grounds."

I paused, trying to keep up with Frankie on the path as my mind whirred. "That's right," I said finally. "Alicia and Sara. It's a veterinarian and an assistant. We met her."

"You met the veterinarian?" demanded Frankie, stopping on the path and giving me an accusatory look. "What did she say?"

I shrugged. "No, actually—we met her assistant.

Sara. She was on the path through the nature preserve when we were exploring the grounds the first night."

Frankie's eyes narrowed. "Did she seem suspicious?"

I didn't know what to say to that. Had Sara seemed suspicious? No, not really. In fact, I could barely remember the few words we'd exchanged with her.

"No," I said after a moment. Frankie sighed, looking disappointed, and continued along the path.

Suddenly it occurred to me how upset Frankie seemed, how awkward and accusatory she had been with Violeta, and what Violeta had just told us. "Oh my gosh . . . wait a minute, Frankie. You don't think Alicia and Sara did this, do you? I mean, this case is far from solved."

Frankie turned on her heel, squinting at me in the late-afternoon sun. "Is it?" she asked. "Think about it, Nancy. We know the person responsible for these events is writing those notes in Cristobal's office. We know that she used an animal tranquilizer *only available to vets* to drug Pedro, and probably gave some to Pretty Boy. We know that the person has, or thinks she has, inside information about Casa Verde that she wants us all to figure out. *Look deeper.*"

"But—but!" I held up my hand. "We have no idea what Alicia or Sara's motive would be! And that completely leaves out the weird tension between Enrique and Cristobal. Plus, doesn't it make sense that the owners of the resort would also have access to whatever drugs Alicia and Sara have in the veterinary office?"

Frankie frowned at me. "Well," she said as we rounded a corner and the small veterinary office came into view, "that's a good question for Alicia, isn't it?"

"I'm sorry," said a petite brunette, her long, straight hair pinned up in a bun and a pink doctor's coat dwarfing her tiny frame. "Who are you again?"

"I'm *Frankie Gundersen*," Frankie replied exasperatedly, as though her name should be as recognizable as James Bond or Hannah Montana. "Of the *New York Globe*?"

The woman looked confused. "This is a newspaper?"

Frankie sighed deeply. "It is a newspaper with a *two-hundred-year history*!" she replied. "Recognized throughout the world! Except, I guess, in some veterinarian's office in the bowels of Central America." She rolled her eyes.

"Um," I spoke up. "My name is Nancy. Are you . . . Alicia?"

The woman's eyes warmed with recognition, as

though one of us was finally saying something that made sense. "Yes! Can I answer any questions about the nature preserve?"

"No," Frankie broke in, impatient, "but you can answer some questions about why Casa Verde's driver was found unconscious yesterday afternoon with tons of midazolam in his blood!"

Alicia's small face crinkled with surprise and concern. "Pedro? Pedro was found with midazolam in his blood?"

I nodded, gesturing to Frankie to cool it for a minute. "You didn't hear about that?" I asked. "It was kind of a freaky incident. I thought Cristobal would tell all the resort employees."

"True," murmured Frankie, tapping her lip again. "That *is* strange, no? You'd think he would warn them that they might be in danger."

I shrugged and turned back to Alicia, who was staring at the floor, stunned. "Cristobal has been very tense about Casa Verde's opening and this press tour," she said, glancing up at me apologetically. "He hasn't exactly been . . . forthcoming lately. Or even around."

That was interesting. "He's seemed tense to you?" I asked, but at the same time, Frankie stomped her foot on the floor and demanded, "How do you think this midazolam got to Pedro? Are you the only person on the resort grounds with access to it?"

Alicia looked from me to Frankie. "I really have no idea," she replied. "We have some here in the office, yes—but Sara and I guard it very carefully. When we're not here, the office is securely locked."

"Does Cristobal have access to that key?" I asked.

Alicia looked at me, clearly surprised at my question. "Yes," she said finally, in a tone that implied she didn't think this was relevant. "But Cristobal would never hurt an employee. He treats us all like family."

Like Enrique? I wondered, remembering Juliana's harsh words the night before: *You're angry at him. And you have every right to be.*

Frankie narrowed her eyes at Alicia. "Who's Sara?" she asked.

"Sara is my assistant," the veterinarian replied. "She—oh, there she is." As she spoke, there was a rustling in the back room, and the girl George, Bess, and I had met on the path stepped into the room, carrying a large water bottle with a metal spout.

Sara looked at Alicia in surprise. *"Me necesita?"*

Alicia gestured at Frankie and me, gently shaking her head. "These guests have come to ask us a few questions. Apparently, there was an incident yesterday—Pedro was drugged with midazolam, and he passed out."

Sara's eyes widened in alarm. She quickly recovered, though, and turned to Frankie and me. "Why are they here?" she asked Alicia. "And not Cristobal?"

Alicia shrugged, looking from Sara to us uncomfortably. "Sara, you know he's been tense lately. He's probably busy asking someone else questions."

Sara nodded, then turned her gaze to us. "I was here all day yesterday," she said simply. "Nobody took any midazolam."

"Well, that's convenient, because we don't think it was done yesterday," Frankie snapped back, a nasty tone entering her voice. "What about the night before?"

"The night before, *I* was here," Alicia broke in, frowning at Frankie. "And Sara's right, nobody took any midazolam. We checked. I'm not sure what you're accusing us of, but we're telling you the truth. We keep an organized office here, and we're very careful about the drugs we use. If someone stole midazolam to use it to ruin your tour—well, they must have done it in the middle of the night, when we weren't around." She paused and took a breath. I could tell that Frankie's pushiness was making her angry, and she was struggling not to lose her temper in front of a guest. Not for the first time, I wished Frankie weren't with me. If I'd been alone, I knew I could have put Alicia and Sara at ease, let them know

I wasn't accusing them, and convinced them to give me all the information they had.

Instead I had a feeling we were about to get kicked out of the office.

I was right.

"I'm sure this incident was upsetting," Alicia went on, "but that's all I can tell you. Please let Cristobal know we're happy to talk to him about any of this, or to go over the details of when we were or were not in the office. But that doesn't seem appropriate to discuss with guests, no matter how sincere I'm sure you are about wanting to find the culprit. I hope you understand." She flashed a brief, and clearly forced, smile.

Frankie's expression went cold—even colder than it had been when she was asking the questions. I had a terrible feeling she was about to make it worse, and I wished I could jump into her mouth and physically stop her from saying—

"And what if *you're* the culprit?" Frankie asked Alicia, with a satisfied smile. "Wouldn't this make a convenient reason to stonewall us? 'Oh, you're just guests, it wouldn't be appropriate.' Well, let me tell you something."

Frankie stepped closer to Alicia and lowered her voice. I cringed.

"I see you coming from a mile away," said Frankie

in a voice just above a whisper. "And if you did this, you can bet Nancy and I are going to figure it out. *Good day.*"

I couldn't say anything else.

"Come on, Nance," Frankie commanded, grabbing my shoulder as she walked by me on the way out. Casting an apologetic glance at Alicia and Sara, I turned and followed her.

"I think that went very well," Frankie said as she briskly walked back up the path to the main building. "Don't you agree?"

I didn't trust anything to come out of my mouth just then, so I nodded. But one thought kept repeating itself in my head.

This is why I only work with people I trust.

FAMILY TIES

Bess and George looked at me sympathetically as we picked at Enrique's arroz con
pollo a few minutes later at dinner. We were
huddled together, me trying to fill them in on my
"investigations" with Frankie as Poppy entertained
the rest of our group with a long story about something Russell Crowe had told her once about mois-
turizers.

"So you didn't learn *anything*?" George asked,
cutting her eyes at Frankie. Frankie seemed to be
in a great mood, laughing it up with the rest of the
group. But then, she thought our whole interview
had gone "very well," and she probably thought it

was just a matter of time before her big-shot *Globe* scientists found Alicia's fingerprints on a bottle of midazolam and we could all kiss this crazy press tour good-bye.

I sighed. "We learned about the midazolam," I replied. "And we learned that it's fast acting—and very dangerous. So we learned that our mystery note writer is willing to hurt people, just like he or she said in the note today."

Bess shuddered. "What do you think the note writer wants?" she asked. "Every note says to 'look deeper'—but at what?"

George shrugged. "Clearly he or she thinks there's some kind of secret that we should know about Casa Verde," she said. "And I'm sure it's no coincidence that this is happening during a *press* tour—so whatever we learned would be broadcast all over the American media."

"Someone is trying to ruin Casa Verde," I agreed. "The question is, why?"

Bess looked thoughtful. "The note that was left when Pretty Boy disappeared—it said something about caring about animals, didn't it?"

I nodded. "'If you really love animals.' That's right. Is it possible that Alicia or Sara know something about animals being mistreated at Casa Verde?"

George wrinkled her nose. "Like what?" she asked.

"Wouldn't that miss the point of being a nature preserve?"

Bess shrugged. "I dunno. Maybe Casa Verde isn't so *verde* after all. Maybe that's what the mystery note writer and dognapper and driver-drugger wants us to figure out."

George shook her head. "The thing is," she said, "I really did a lot of research about this. When I won this trip, I was skeptical. I didn't want to go to some trendy place that was really responsible for tromping tourists through the rain forest and killing it, you know? All my research told me that Casa Verde really is a state-of-the-art green resort—that they've actually won some award from the Costa Rican government for their green initiatives. I mean, this is all from when the resort was being planned, but being here, it really looks just like the plans said."

Bess sighed, throwing up her hands. "Then I'm stumped," she said. "If Casa Verde convinced my skeptic cousin they're green enough, then they must be green enough. But if that's the case, what can this person want?"

"I think we know what they want," I replied. "They want the resort to fail. The question is *why*."

George watched my face curiously. "You still think there's something between the Arrojo brothers, don't you?"

"But why would they ruin their own resort's chances?" asked Bess.

"I'm not sure," I admitted. "But I think the only force strong enough to make someone ruin their own investment is love."

"Thanks for another amazing dinner, Enrique," Bess said as the three of us carried our dirty dishes into the kitchen.

Enrique was typing on a small desktop computer set up on a card table in the corner, and he looked up at us in surprise. "Oh . . . girls! Why are you bringing your own plates? You should have gotten Juliana, she's just working on some homework in the lobby."

"That's okay. We all have arms," I said with a smile. "We can carry our own plates. Besides, isn't that a big part of the green movement—that everyone has to chip in?"

Enrique smiled warmly. "Yes, I think you're right about that."

"Is that a computer?" George asked suddenly, in much the same tone Robin had used when talking about the horses. I'd forgotten that George had gone four whole days now without computer access.

Enrique stood up, blushing. "Yes, this is my little baby," he replied. "Nothing fancy, but it keeps me up on soccer scores and finds me new recipes."

"Can I use it?" begged George, and it seemed to me she was practically salivating. "I don't mean to beg, but—I'm going through withdrawal. I haven't seen my e-mail in days!"

Enrique didn't quite look like he understood, but he nodded quickly. "Of course, of course!" he said, stepping away from the card table. "Please, be my guest. Any time you like."

Before running over to the computer, though, George suddenly gripped my arm. "Come on, Nance," she said in a low voice. I glanced at her, and she winked at me. Unsure what she meant, I followed her to the computer.

"Nance and I have this endless crossword puzzle going on," George explained to Enrique, who didn't seem to know what she was talking about. Actually, I didn't either. I'd recently investigated a case of cyberbullying that had gotten way out of hand, and I now preferred to live my life offline, thank you very much.

George sat down at the table, then gave me a meaningful look. She clicked on the browser icon, but instead of typing in the URL or her e-mail's website, she went up to the menu and selected "Internet history." I felt little prickles of excitement running up and down my arms. George was checking out the sites Enrique had visited! She was getting to be a good actress—she'd totally fooled me with her "Internet withdrawal."

She'd apparently fooled Bess, too. "My cousin is hopelessly addicted to technology," she explained to Enrique, shaking her head. "But so much outdated technology ends up in landfills!"

Enrique nodded, his eyes widening as he warmed to the topic. "Or worse than landfills! Many outdated computers end up in third-world countries, where people destroy their environment with harsh chemicals, trying to extract any valuable substances."

Bess nodded. "I heard about that on *Dateline*. It's so terrible. These companies are promising to recycle technological waste, and they're just feeding this terrible system!"

George suddenly grabbed my wrist. I bent to look at the computer monitor, and she silently pointed: She was on a website called The Truth About Pharmaceuticals. The entry she pointed to was labeled "Midazolam: proper doses and usage." Under "Dosage," she was pointing to the line "Should never administer more than 0.2 mg per pound. A dosage of 30 mg would put down most human subjects for two to three hours . . ."

I turned to George with wide eyes. What possible reason could Enrique have for visiting a pharmaceutical site? And what were the chances he just happened on this entry that gave precise instructions for how much midazolam would knock out a human . . . in the very room where Pedro's water bottle was probably drugged?

George reached up and tapped a line at the top of the browser. *Visited at 8:46 p.m., Tuesday.* That was the night before we'd gone to La Paz Waterfall Gardens . . . the night when Pedro's water was likely drugged.

I gulped. Was it possible? Could our mystery note writer, dognapper, and driver-drugger be the quiet, mild-mannered Enrique? Could whatever Enrique had against his brother be enough for him to risk financial ruin and innocent lives to see his business fail? And if it was Enrique—if Enrique was the person brazen enough to drug a driver's drink before he got behind the wheel—then what else did he have up his sleeve? With a sick feeling, I realized that we'd been eating Enrique's cooking all week. If he had drugged Pedro's water bottle, what might he sneak into our food?

George looked at me, just as wide-eyed and alarmed as I felt, and started clicking on the desktop files. Bills for food deliveries . . . a Christmas card list . . . and a file full of personal photos.

"Oh, I *only* drink organic milk now," Bess was saying. "All those hormones!"

George scrolled through the folder. Vacation

photos of Enrique and Juliana, a photo of Juliana as a little kid at what looked like a dance recital . . . she kept scrolling down . . .

"And fast food!" Bess was saying. "Don't even get me started on fast food!"

"Oh my God!"

We all jumped at the outburst from George—and all of us, even Enrique and Bess, suddenly turned to face her.

"I'm sorry," George whispered, but she grabbed my arm and gestured wildly at the computer screen. Onscreen was an old wedding photograph—old enough that it had clearly yellowed and worn, and must have been scanned into the computer in its beat-up state. But in it, a man and a woman, dressed in the super-glitzy wedding fashions of the 1980s, smiled at the camera in front of a cheesy sunset background. The man, though much younger and thinner, and with more hair, was clearly Enrique. And the woman . . .

I gasped, looking at the screen.

The woman was Virginia Arrojo.

Cristobal's wife!

THE REAL CULPRIT

When I spotted the wedding photo of Enrique and Cristobal, several things happened at once. First, Enrique seemed to realize that George and I weren't checking e-mail, and he came running over to the computer. When he spotted his old wedding picture, his face fell, and he began turning a deep shade of red.

"WHAT ON EARTH ARE YOU DOING?" he shouted loud enough to wake the neighbors—in Panama.

Too stunned to move, George and I just sat there, staring at what we'd found. Within seconds, the other guests began to run in from the dining room.

"George! Nancy! What's going on?" demanded Hildy, placing a protective hand on Robin's shoulder.

Frankie came running in after her, followed by Sarene, and her eyes lit up when she saw George and me sitting in front of the computer, with Enrique freaking out.

"Excuse me," she commanded, slipping past the other guests and pushing Enrique roughly to the side. She stood behind me, looking over my shoulder at the computer screen, and gasped.

Frankie's presence seemed to bring George back to life. She clicked on the Internet browser, scrolling through the pages we'd found.

"He looked up dosages for midazolam," George told her in a disbelieving voice. "On Tuesday. And then there's this picture. . . ."

Frankie shook her head. "Wow. Wow." She looked from the computer screen to Enrique. He looked so miserable, so utterly shaken, that for a moment I actually felt terrible about snooping on him. Until I realized that his petty jealousy of his brother had cost us all our luggage, a dog—and nearly our lives. It was just dumb luck that none of us had gotten hurt in the La Paz or horseback-riding incidents.

As I was thinking all this, it seemed, Frankie was working herself up for the performance of a lifetime.

"Ladies and gentlemen," she announced gravely, pointing a straight, accusatory finger at Enrique's chest, *"I give you your saboteur!"*

"What?!" echoed through the crowd, and Robin loudly asked her mother, "What's a sa–boe–terr?" On the other end of Frankie's finger, though, Enrique shook off his stupor and began to look stunned.

"Qué?" he asked.

"You were so jealous that your brother stole the woman you loved that *you stole our luggage!*" Frankie went on in her loud, theatrical voice.

Sarene, who was standing near the doorway, suddenly gasped and stepped forward. "That means you also put that threatening note on our door!" she cried, pointing at Enrique.

And then Kat, who I'd barely noticed in her quiet state, came alive and marched over to Enrique, shoving her finger into his chest. "You dognapped Pretty Boy! Where is he? *Where is he?!*" she demanded, her voice rising into a shriek.

Just then Cristobal entered the kitchen, which meant that our shouts were loud enough that he must have heard them in his family's apartment. He took one look at the chaos and his eyes widened, but within seconds he'd pasted on that calm, smooth, "this will all be fine" smile that I'd come to know so well.

"Calm down, calm down," he urged the crowd. "What's going on here?"

Nobody listened to him.

"You creep!" Poppy was yelling at Enrique. "I had seven hundred fifty dollars' worth of shoes in my luggage!"

In all the chaos, I looked toward the door and suddenly noticed another face in the crowd—just as stunned, but perhaps for different reasons from everyone else. Juliana stood in the doorway, her mouth open, her expression stricken. She looked horrified, but there was another emotion in her eyes too. It took me a minute to identify it. Could it be—guilt?

"*Dios mio!*" Everyone around me was shouting now, so I saw Juliana's lips form the words rather than heard them. With that, she took off running. She darted from the doorway, and I heard her light footsteps run through the dining hall and into the lobby, toward the back door that led to the gardens.

I hesitated for only a second. Then, placing a hand on George's shoulder and murmuring a quick "Give me a minute," I ran out of the kitchen too. I raced through the dining room, through the lobby, and out the door that led to the pathways through the gardens, which by now I'd explored more times than I'd ever wanted to.

I ran down the pathway, away from the main

building, through the gardens with their heady floral scents and into the very beginning of the nature preserve. Already I was panting, and I hadn't caught even a glimpse of Juliana. Where had she gone? And how long would I have to chase her?

As I paused on a narrow bridge to get my bearings, I heard a sniffling sound from the forest. Looking over to my right, I saw a stream wending its way under a huge tree, covered by a tangle of vines—and beneath, something bright red. As my eyes adjusted to the dim evening light, I could just make out Juliana, in her red T-shirt, sitting under the tree and crying into her hands.

Slowly I moved off the path and approached her.

"Juliana," I said softly, standing before her. I wasn't sure whether she'd seen me come after her, or even had any idea that someone had been following her.

When she heard me, she gulped loudly and swiped tears out of her eyes to look up at me. "Oh," she said simply. "It's you, Nancy."

I nodded, gently kneeling down and trying to settle myself next to her on the ground. "Want to talk?"

She let out a short, sharp laugh. "About how messed-up my family is? Not really." She paused, wiping more tears away, and then looked down into her lap. "What kind of person would do that to his own brother?"

I nodded sympathetically. I hadn't been sure how

many of the accusations she'd heard, but I guessed she had put together that her father was responsible for trying to sabotage our press tour. "Do you think he'd been planning this for a long time?" I asked. "Helping Cristobal get the resort ready, but at the same time, planning to sabotage their investment the minute it opened?"

Juliana looked at me, her eyes wide and uncomprehending. "What?"

I looked at her. "You know," I said encouragingly. "All these incidents your father planned to ruin our press tour and make the journalists write about what a disaster their stay was."

Juliana furrowed her brow. "Is that what you think my father did?" she asked.

I frowned. "I'm sorry. What were you talking about—what someone could do to his own brother?"

She looked at me like I was very dense. "My uncle Cristobal stole away his own brother's *wife*," she replied, shaking her head. "Can you imagine doing that to anybody—much less your own brother?"

I bit my lip, thinking back to what I'd heard in Cristobal's office. *You're angry at him. And you're even angrier at her. And you have every right to be.* Clearly Juliana knew about her family's odd history—and she wasn't any happier about it than Enrique.

I felt my heart drop into my stomach. "Juliana,"

I said quietly, "could you tell me what exactly happened between your father, Virginia, and Cristobal?"

"Sure." Juliana nodded resolutely, taking a deep breath. "Virginia and my father were high school sweethearts. They were crazy about each other, and as soon as they graduated, my father asked Virginia to marry him—even though they would have to live apart while she attended college. She said yes, and they were married just before she left for the university."

I nodded. "Okay."

Juliana's face darkened. "My uncle Cristobal was studying at the university as well. He began 'looking out' for Virginia—meeting her for meals, studying with her, walking her to classes." She frowned. "Soon they began to have feelings for each other. My uncle Cristobal, you know—he can be very charming."

I thought back to our initial meeting with Cristobal at the airport. I could definitely see it being hard to spend lots of time with him without the thought of romance at least occurring to you.

"My father had no idea any of this was going on," Juliana continued. "He still talks about those days, being right out of school and married to Virginia. He says he's never been happier. He was totally in love with her, and he thought she felt the same way."

I could see where this story was going. "But," I prompted her.

"But," Juliana went on, meeting my eyes, "at Christmas break, Virginia admitted to my father that she'd developed feelings for Cristobal. And she said her feelings for him were stronger than she'd ever had for my father." She paused, her eyes wet with sympathy. "She wanted an annulment so she could marry Cristobal. My father, as you might imagine, was crushed."

I nodded, feeling terrible for Enrique. I could only imagine how hard it would be to lose young love like that—and worse, to lose it to your own brother! Cristobal had always seemed like such a nice person, but how could he have stolen his brother's wife away? It was hard to wrap my head around.

A thought suddenly occurred to me. "Juliana, she's not—is Virginia your *mother*?" I asked, horrified to imagine how this all must affect Juliana if it were the case.

Juliana shook her head grimly. "No, no," she insisted. "My mother came later. They married years after Virginia. They didn't work out either. I think my father was still hung up on Virginia."

"And Cristobal? What's his take on all this?"

Juliana rolled her eyes. "You know Cristobal. He's handsome, he's charming—he gets away with everything. He felt terrible, he said, and he spent years trying to make it up to my father. He paid for my father to go to cooking school, and then got him a job at a fancy hotel he was managing in San José. But my uncle doesn't understand—you can't undo something like this."

I nodded. "How do you get along with Cristobal?"

Juliana shrugged. "Oh, you know. Okay. He's my uncle. And I do love him—of course I do. I just have a really hard time forgiving him for this." The corners of her mouth turned down. "Especially since I know my father never got over it."

I tilted my head. "What makes you think that?"

Juliana laughed darkly. "Everything," she replied. "When my father sees Cristobal and Virginia together, even to this day, he's in a bad mood for days afterward. After my mother, he never remarried—and he still talks about Aunt Virginia like she's the most amazing woman on earth. He's always saying how smart she is, how beautiful, what a good mother. And worse . . ."

She paused and looked around, as though she were worried about someone overhearing. But the only living souls around us were a bunch of monkeys and lizards. "I've found the love letters he writes her on his computer."

"Love letters?" I asked in surprise. I guessed George had missed that folder.

Juliana nodded. "They don't have a name on them, but you can tell who he's talking about. I don't think he ever sends them. I think they're just a place for him to write down his feelings."

"Wow," I breathed. There was no denying it: This was one crazy family secret. It amazed me that Enrique and Cristobal were even still speaking, never mind in business together.

"Well," I said finally, reaching out to touch Juliana's shoulder, "this all must be very hard for your father to deal with, and I'm sure it's hard for you to watch. But it was still wrong for you to do what you did."

Juliana's eyes flickered in surprise. "What?" she demanded.

"You know," I said, trying to sound friendly and understanding. "Stealing all our luggage and hiding it in the forest. Drugging Pedro and dognapping Pretty Boy. Frightening our horses yesterday. And sending all those notes."

Juliana's eyes, which had previously been friendly and eager to share, suddenly turned panicked. "I didn't do any of those things!"

I gave her a hard look. "Come on, Juliana. You know the hotel grounds. You had access to our luggage and to the hotel stationery the notes were written on, and I'm sure you could have borrowed your father's keys to get your hands on the drug that was given to Pedro. You knew exactly where we were going to be every day, and for how long."

I looked at Juliana, and she stared back, hard. The fear in her eyes was turning to anger.

"I know you were angry at Cristobal," I went on, "but in trying to hurt him, you hurt a lot of innocent people—including your own father. Did you forget that he'll lose money too if Casa Verde fails?"

"I didn't do any of those things!" Juliana repeated, more strongly this time.

I looked at her dubiously. "Juliana, I saw the look on your face when everyone was piling on your father back there. It wasn't just anger or frustration. It was guilt—because you knew he was getting blamed for your actions."

"That's not true!" Juliana insisted, her eyes blazing now. "I was upset, yes, but only because I was afraid my father was getting in trouble! And so what if he *did* do all the things you accused him of? I love Cristobal, but he had it coming. Someday he deserves to find out what it feels like to lose!"

I nodded. "Juliana, that sounds a lot like a confession."

She glared at me. "You can't prove that I did it. Because I didn't."

I sighed, getting to my feet. "Actually, I can."

Juliana's face dropped.

"There's one variable in all this that we haven't figured out yet," I went on. "What happened to Pretty

Boy. And I'm guessing, because you seem like a moral person who has sympathy for animals, you wouldn't hurt him. I'm guessing you would keep him somewhere."

Juliana frowned. "I don't know what you're talking about. I didn't even like that little ankle-biting dog."

"Well, if that's the case," I offered, "then you'll have no problem with me looking in your study room."

Back at the main building, a shouting match was still going on in the kitchen.

"How do I *know* that?" Frankie was yelling at Enrique. "How do I *know* you had nothing to do with my hair dryer going missing?"

I was dismayed by the chaos—and especially by my own role in involving Frankie, who seemed to be the ringmaster—but at the same time, it allowed me to quietly get Cristobal's attention without alerting any of the other guests to what was going on.

"Cristobal," I whispered, tugging on his sleeve as he watched the shouting from the kitchen doorway (I wondered how long it had taken him to give up on calming everybody down), "we need your help."

On the way out of the building and down the walk by the pool to the room Juliana used to study, I explained my suspicions to Cristobal, and how Juliana had agreed to let us look in her room.

Cristobal looked at his niece in shock. "Juliana," he said, "this is all a big joke, no?"

When she wouldn't respond and just stared stonily down at the ground, Cristobal turned to me. "This is a mistake," he insisted. "My niece would never do something like this."

"I certainly hope that's the case," I replied honestly. "But I think we need to check." I paused. "Maybe it *isn't* her. Maybe it's . . . where are your investigations leading, Cristobal?"

Cristobal sighed and shook his head, looking defeated. "The truth is, Nancy . . ." He paused, like this pained him to admit. "The truth is I don't know. I don't have any idea. This person seems to want to hurt me, or hurt Casa Verde, and I can't think of who would want to hurt me."

I nodded, not speaking the obvious truth. Cristobal was a man who was used to getting along with everybody. He didn't know what it felt like to have enemies, to feel like anyone wasn't on his side. But if my hunches were correct, he *did* have enemies—and they were right within his own family. A small part of me sincerely hoped we'd find nothing in Juliana's study room but books and pencils.

Finally we reached the room. Juliana refused to

meet our eyes, nibbling on a fingernail and staring down at the ground as Cristobal used his manager's key to open the door.

"Yip!" We all startled at a short, sharp bark. "Yip! Yip yip yip yip!"

As we were assaulted by a torrent of angry Chihuahua barking, I could just make out a familiar small yellow dog sitting on a pillow in the center of the room. In front of him was a plate with a recently well-chewed steak bone. In the corner, someone had thoughtfully turned on a television and set it to a Spanish version of *The Dog Whisperer.*

Juliana looked into the room, stunned for a moment, and then resigned. "I didn't do this," she insisted, turning from me to her uncle. "Uncle Cristobal, I swear . . ."

But Cristobal, who looked stunned himself, seemed to close off his emotions as he shook his head. "You did, Juliana," he said sadly. "You did."

A few minutes later, Cristobal, Juliana, and I returned to the kitchen, where I practically launched the extremely bitey Chihuahua back into the arms of his owner. "Kat," I said, giving her a heads-up, "look who we found!"

Kat's blue eyes widened to the size of marbles, and then she dissolved into tears. "Oh my God, Pretty

Boy!" she cried. "Nancy! Oh my God! He's naked! Where did you *find* him?"

Out of the corner of my eye, I saw Cristobal pull Juliana by the arm over to her father, where he whispered something in Enrique's ear. Enrique's eyes widened in shock and recognition, and he stared at his daughter.

"Excuse us," Cristobal called to us guests, backing out of the room with his brother and niece. "We need to have a private conversation."

As everyone gathered around Kat and Pretty Boy, and people began pelting questions at me—especially Bess and George, who had no idea that I'd even suspected Juliana—I slowly explained what had happened in the last few minutes, and how I'd come to the conclusion that it was Juliana, and not her father, who'd sabotaged our press tour to get back at Cristobal.

"Wow," breathed Hildy, shaking her head as she reached out to pat Pretty Boy (who promptly bit her). "You're quite the sleuth, aren't you?"

"Absolutely," agreed Frankie, suddenly sliding over to me and wrapping her arm around my shoulders. "You know, kid, you're not so bad. In fact, you'd make a heck of an investigative journalist. Look what a great help you were to me in solving this mystery!"

POSTCARD FROM COSTA RICA

THE NEW YORK GLOBE
Sunday edition

POSTCARD FROM COSTA RICA: THINGS NOT SO ROSY AT CASA VERDE
By Frankie Gundersen

SAN JOSÉ—For many entrepreneurs, the first rule of going into business with family members might be: Don't tick anyone off. This is a lesson that Cristobal Arrojo, co-owner and manager of the Casa Verde state-of-the-art eco-resort in San Isidro, Costa Rica, has learned the hard way. Twenty years ago, Arrojo, now forty-three, shamelessly flirted with and eventually stole the affection of his brother's wife, Virginia. Now it seems that this trespass almost cost him the millions of dollars spent on building his new resort.

Globe reporter Frankie Gundersen is among the many journalists currently staying at Casa Verde for a press tour. Things began to look fishy when Gundersen's luggage, and the luggage of all of her cotravelers, disappeared soon after their arrival. Things looked even more suspicious when some associates of Gundersen's found the luggage destroyed in the resort's extensive nature preserve. And they got worse when threatening notes were left on the door of the room Gundersen shared with her friend, National Book Award–winning author Sarene Neuman, and other places where they were found by the guests.

But it seems that whoever was trying to sabotage the press tour wasn't aware that one of the country's most renowned investigative journalists, with the power of the legendary New York Globe behind her, was on the case. With just a bit of assistance from fellow travelers, Gundersen soon got to the bottom of the sabotage—which, you might say, was caused by a green-eyed monster. . . .

"Wow," Bess said with a sigh, leaning back on the headrest of her seat on the bus as we pulled back into the driveway of Casa Verde. "That was actually *insanely* relaxing."

"It was," George agreed, looking dreamily out the window. "I feel like I just took a three-hour nap."

I grinned. "Well, it probably didn't hurt that Adam and Sarene stayed behind."

"You can say that again," Bess agreed with a chuckle. "Is it just me, or are Adam and Poppy fighting all the time lately?"

"Not *all* the time," George said snarkily. "There was at least ten minutes at dinner last night when their mouths were too full to argue."

I sighed. It was true—Adam and Poppy had disrupted several meals and trips in the last few days with their sniping. Poppy had been much more mellow and friendly today, without her beau. "And Sarene," I said, trying to put her peculiar personality into words, "isn't exactly a barrel of laughs." Over the last few days, it seemed she was finding fault with everything the tour group did. Buying souvenirs exploited the indigenous people of Costa Rica. And snorkeling brought destructive tourists into protected areas of ocean, eventually destroying the natural coral reefs.

George closed her eyes and shook her head. "Let's forget all this negativity and get back to the trip. I've never been snorkeling before! It really is like entering another world, this whole separate world under the surface of the water. . . ."

I smirked. "You're just feeling all sentimental because we were lucky enough to see a sea turtle."

George's head snapped up, and she grinned. "You know they're endangered, right? Hawaiians believe that the sea turtles have great power and wisdom. It's not just coincidence that we ran into that turtle, guys. It was a *blessing*."

Bess smiled. "Well, we could probably use a little blessing after the events of the last few days."

George groaned. "I know," she agreed. "I still can't believe that crazy article Frankie wrote. She took total credit for solving the case!"

"It wasn't exactly a surprise," I admitted. "Besides, I'm just glad all that craziness is over. Kat's back to her old self now that Pretty Boy is back, and Cristobal told me that he, Enrique, and Juliana are seeing a counselor."

Bess nodded. "I kind of miss seeing her at our meals, but I'm sure it's for the best that she's not working at Casa Verde right now."

"And George and I saw Alicia on our hike yesterday morning. She says they have totally new procedures now for locking up the drugs at night so no nonveterinary personnel can touch them."

George looked thoughtful. "Did they ever figure out how exactly Juliana got the tranquilizer?"

I shook my head. "No. Nobody saw her. But we

figure she must have just gone down there late one night while her dad was working and thought she was studying. It would have been really easy for her to get his key for an hour or so."

Bess sighed, shaking her head. "I still can't believe she would try something as dangerous as drugging our driver. It just doesn't seem like her."

I shrugged. "True, but everyone is capable of crazy things when they feel their family is threatened. We're just lucky everyone came out of it okay."

The bus pulled up in front of the lobby entrance, and Cristobal jumped out, helping all of us down the steps.

"All right, everybody!" he cried. "Coffee is available in the dining room, and you all have about an hour before dinner to shower, nap, swim, whatever you like."

I smiled at my friends as we waited to get off the bus. "Now *this*," I told them, "is what a vacation should feel like. I can't believe we have to leave in three days."

Everyone seemed to be moving in blissful slow motion as they walked into the lobby, Hildy and Robin in the lead. Suddenly, as I was just stepping off the bus, a shrill scream pierced the air.

"Mommy! What is it?"

It was Robin!

There was a mad rush as everyone tried to squeeze into the lobby to see what had frightened Robin so. Frankie pushed hardest, of course—and since I knew what to expect of her by now, I followed along in her wake and easily got into the lobby, where I was stunned by what I saw.

Blood. There was blood everywhere, staining the carpet a deep crimson. In the center of the lobby, in a limp, smelly heap, was—

I couldn't believe it.

It was a dead sea turtle.

A dead *endangered* sea turtle.

"*Dios mio,*" Cristobal murmured behind me, stepping into the lobby in shock. "What have they done?"

Sitting on top of the bloody turtle was a note—in familiar block handwriting. Since everyone seemed to be too stunned to move, I finally forced myself forward toward the turtle, and, trying not to look down, I grabbed the note off its chest. Sticky, dark blood clung to the note in places, but I darted away from the corpse and took the note back to my tour mates.

I TOLD YOU TO LOOK DEEPER. HOW
MUCH MONEY HAS CASA VERDE TAKEN
FROM THE GOVERNMENT, ONLY TO

HURT WHAT THEY ARE SUPPOSED TO
CONSERVE? UNLESS YOU WANT MORE
ANIMALS TO SUFFER LIKE THIS, FIND
THE TRUTH!!

"Oh my God," breathed Frankie, staring over my shoulder at the angry words. "There's no way Juliana could have done this. She was supposed to be in school all day today. That means it's not over."

"No," I agreed, shaking my head. "And whoever this is just killed a revered, endangered creature." I paused. "Who knows what he or she must be willing to do to us!"

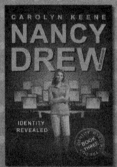

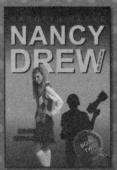

FRANKLIN W. DIXON

THE HARDY BOYS

Undercover Brothers®

INVESTIGATE THESE TWO ADVENTUROUS MYSTERY TRILOGIES WITH AGENTS FRANK AND JOE HARDY!

#25 Double Trouble

#26 Double Down

#28 Galaxy X

#29 X-plosion

#27 Double Deception

#30 The X-Factor

From Aladdin
Published by Simon & Schuster

Read these books by
Marlene Wallach

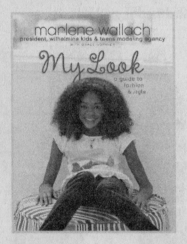

Collect them all!